MYSTERY

THE FATE OF PRINCES

THE FATE OF PRINCES

P. C. DOHERTY

St. Martin's Press
New York

Library of Congress Cataloging-in-Publication Data

Doherty, P. C.
   The fate of princes / P. C. Doherty.
      p.   cm.
   ISBN 0-312-05429-7
 ⋰ 1. Richard III, King of England, 1452-1485—Fiction. ⋰ I. Title.
PR6054.037F38   1991
823'.914—dc20   90-19518
                                                       CIP

First published in Great Britain by Robert Hale Limited.

First U.S. Edition: March 1991
10 9 8 7 6 5 4 3 2 1

To my wife, Carla

List of Personages Mentioned

Edward IV, King of England 1461 – 1483

Richard III, King of England 1483 – 1485

Elizabeth Woodville, Edward IV's Queen (formerly the widow of Lord Grey)

Edward and Richard the two sons of Edward IV and Elizabeth Woodville, commonly known as 'the Princes in the Tower'

Elizabeth of York eldest daughter of Edward IV

George, Duke of Clarence brother to Edward IV and Richard III, destroyed by the Woodville faction

Margaret, Duchess of Burgundy sister to Edward IV and Richard III

Lord William Hastings close friend and chamberlain of Edward IV

John Morton, Bishop of Ely, an inveterate Lancastrian seized during Richard's coup in 1483 and handed over to the Duke of Buckingham for safe keeping.

Margaret Beaufort, mother of Henry Tudor (later Henry VII) at the time of this novel married to Lord Thomas Stanley, a powerful landowner.

Francis, Viscount Lovell, Richard III's chamberlain and close friend.

Sir Robert Brackenbury, Constable of the Tower of London during Richard's reign.

Henry Stafford, Duke of Buckingham, married to one

of Elizabeth Woodville's daughters. He reputedly
hated the Woodville faction and was Richard III's
strongest adherent in the coup of 1483.

Earl Rivers, Elizabeth Woodville's brother and guardian
of the Prince of Wales.

John Howard, Duke of Norfolk (Jack of Norfolk)
Richard III's most powerful ally.

Sir Richard Ratcliffe, Sir James Tyrrell, Sir William
Catesby and Sir Edward Brampton – members of
Richard III's secret council.

Introduction

Fifteenth century England was dominated by a savage, bloody civil war between the Houses of York and Lancaster. The source of this conflict was the weak-willed, ineffectual Henry VI who had neither the energy nor aptitude for rule. Instead, the government was dominated by his strong-minded wife, Margaret of Anjou, aided and abetted by the Duke of Somerset, who held the kingdom in the hope that one day Henry VI's young son, Edward, would continue the Lancastrian line.

In the 1450s the powerful Richard, Duke of York, supported by the Earl of Warwick and other Yorkist war lords, challenged the Lancastrian right to rule, putting forward his own claim to the throne. A series of vicious battles took place; Richard, Duke of York, was killed outside Wakefield but the war was continued by his able brood of sons: Edward (later Edward IV), George, (later Duke of Clarence) and Richard (later Duke of Gloucester and Richard III). Edward of York proved to be a brilliant general. Although he later quarrelled with Warwick (who went over to the House of Lancaster) Edward IV decisively destroyed Lancastrian fortunes in two great battles in 1471: at Barnet just north of London and Tewkesbury in the west. Margaret of Anjou was taken prisoner and her son killed at Tewkesbury, Warwick died at Barnet and Henry VI mysteriously perished in the Tower of London.

Edward settled down to rule. The only threats he faced were those posed by his younger brother George, Duke of Clarence, who resented the growing influence of Edward's queen, Elizabeth Woodville. A widow, formerly married to Lord Grey, Elizabeth had sons by her first marriage and allowed her brother, Anthony Grey, Earl Rivers, and other members of her large, extended family to secure high office and sources of patronage, as well as Clarence's downfall, for he was judiciously murdered in the Tower, leaving the Woodville faction supreme.

Although Edward IV had his mistresses, Elizabeth Woodville had borne him two young princes (Edward and Richard) and a bevy of daughters. Edward IV's brother, Richard, Duke of Gloucester, continued to be loyal, serving his brother in the north and on the Scottish march. Suddenly, in April 1483, Edward IV died of a mysterious illness. The Woodvilles dominated the council whilst Elizabeth's brother, Earl Rivers, controlled the young Prince Edward, the heir-apparent. Their only opponent was Richard of Gloucester who knew the Woodvilles hated him.

In the early summer of 1483 Richard, aided and abetted by Henry Stafford, Duke of Buckingham, staged a brilliant coup d'état. They both invited Earl Rivers to a conference at Stony Stratford but there, Rivers and his companions were arrested and the young Prince Edward was taken by his Uncle Richard who now marched on London. The Woodvilles fled in panic, the Queen to Westminster Abbey, others more fortunate across the seas where the only remaining Lancastrian claimant, Henry Tudor, lived in penurious exile. Richard arrived in London with his own council. Any who opposed him were ruthlessly removed, including Lord William Hastings, Edward IV's old friend and chamberlain. Richard then proclaimed how his dead brother's marriage to Elizabeth Woodville was bigamous as his brother had been betrothed to Lady Eleanor Butler. Consequently, his own nephews were bastards and could not succeed to the throne; Richard had himself crowned whilst his young nephews disappeared into the cold fastness of the Tower of London.

The true nature of Richard's character and the fate of these Princes has always fascinated historians. This dramatic novel, based on documentary evidence, solves not only these mysteries but that of Francis, Viscount Lovell, one of Richard's closest friends, who was last seen fleeing the battle of East Stoke in 1487.

One

Where do I begin? How does one describe and plumb the depths of an evil mystery? One which has grown wild like a briar bush up the walls, along the ground, ready to trip all who come close. So it is with my story. Perhaps it will not glimpse the light of day or have its truths proclaimed for the world to see and hear. I talk about the fate of princes, evil acts in dark, sombre places. Perhaps I should just sit and write while my strength lasts. I, Francis Lovell, Viscount, Chief Butler and Chamberlain of England, the friend and special envoy of Richard III; I, who fought for him at Bosworth and again at East Stoke. Now, locked in the darkness, the certainty of death facing me, I have no other task, no other duty but to tell the truth. But not with hindsight. Oh, no! Truthfully, as events unfurled, like one reads a manuscript, moving from one page to the next.

So where shall I begin? Perhaps here in Minster Lovell. In that late golden summer of 1483 with the early morning sun streaming through the windows of the great hall. I, still bleary-eyed, standing at the doorway, watching King Richard sitting before an empty fire, slouched in a high-backed chair, my favourite, with its black embroidered silk head and arm-rests. He just sat there in his dark-purple hose and red doublet, open at the neck, showing the lace of a cambric shirt, one hand, heavily jewelled, pressed against the russet hair. His face pale and pinched, with thin, bloodless lips, the King looked like some stealthy fox brought to bay by a huntsman. For some strange reason I felt vexed at the ease with which he slouched in my hall. I forgot he was crowned only a few weeks earlier, anointed with holy oil and adorned with crown, orb and sceptre, as he was proclaimed England's new King amidst the heavy clouds of incense and the glorious chants of the choir of Westminster Abbey.

I could not, must not forget that Richard was now King of this realm. I must not think about Hastings' body tossed beside a log in the Tower courtyard, the head rolled off like a ball, just lying there in a pool of dark crimson blood. No, I must not think of that. Or of the two Princes, his brother's children, bastards maybe, but locked away in the cold Tower, and their mother, the witch bitch, Elizabeth Woodville, in sanctuary at Westminster. Yet, on that morning, despite the golden sun, I felt the hall was crowded by ghosts: Richard's brother, gorgeous, golden-haired George of Clarence, mysteriously done to death, his body now mouldering beneath his marble tomb near the high altar of Tewkesbury Abbey; the Earl of Rivers, Woodville's brother, the greatest knight of his age, the guardian of the two small princes – a man of fleshly lusts, who tried to curb them with a hair shirt but God was not appeased. Richard had Rivers arrested and sent to the headsman's block. I had to remember Richard was King, that the death of Rivers and others was necessary. If not, the Woodvilles would have closed in like a pack of dogs and torn him to pieces. They say the dead live in another world, but I think they are constantly with us and Richard was never alone. His enemies were always with him. The living plagued his days and I believe at night the dead crowded round him to sing their mournful vespers.

I wondered if I should leave, return to Anne, my wife, warm and welcoming in our great bed in the chamber above. As I turned, the King called out:

'Francis! Francis! You are not leaving without wishing me a fair day?' I looked back. Richard's face was now transformed by a lopsided smile. He was vulnerable, like the young boy I had played with at Middleham Castle. We were both pages to the great Richard Neville, Earl of Warwick, the soi-disant kingmaker, killed at Barnet, fleeing from a battle he never wished to fight.

'Your Grace,' I replied merrily, 'you seem so sad?' The King brought up his other hand, hidden on the far side of the chair, and I saw the slip of parchment which started our descent into hell.

'What is it, your Grace?'

'What is it, your Grace?' Richard mimicked spitefully. His smile had not reached the hard green eyes, which blazed with a subdued fury. He lifted the parchment up again.

'This, Francis, is our fate. The undoing of ourselves.' He sighed and dropped the paper into his lap. 'Francis, we are finished.'

'What does it say, your Grace?'

'Not much, but everything,' Richard replied. 'It's from Brackenbury.' I stared at the King. I knew Sir Robert well; small, dark, fierce, one of the King's most loyal followers and also Constable of the Tower of London. The very thought made my throat go dry. My stomach lurched as it does when I see a dead man or some fearful phantasm of the night. Now the sunlight, as well as the warmth, disappeared. The hall became an icy stage and I and Richard III of England were the only creatures under the sun. The wheel of fortune, the whirl of politics, the hustle and bustle of unbounding ambition were reduced to this: two men in a hall and the nightmare between them, unspoken and indescribable. Is it not strange how the greatest terrors are those which cannot be explained? Yet they clutch your heart with an iron grip and threaten to stifle the breath in your throat.

'What is it?' I whispered hoarsely.

'The Princes,' Richard muttered, looking away. 'They have gone!'

'In God's sweet name, Richard!' I bellowed, forgetting all his honours and sacred titles. 'What do you mean, gone? Where, for the sake of the sweet Christ, tell me?'

Richard turned, slowly, like a man does in a dream, or beneath the river when he swims against the current. Slowly. Dreadfully. I knew there was a lie, an abominable lie, in what he said.

'The Princes have gone,' he said quietly. 'Vanished! No one knows where.'

I slumped onto a bench running alongside a trestle-table.

'The Princes were guarded,' I said bleakly. 'Guarded by Brackenbury in the White Tower.' My voice rose. 'In God's name, your Grace, they cannot vanish! Have you ...?' I stopped: the accusation hung between us aimed like some mythical dagger at the heart of Richard's crown. The King glared back, one hand up in a threatening gesture, his green narrow eyes hooded and secretive.

'Have I killed them? Is that what you're saying, Francis? Will you join the whisperers? The secretive ones who skulk behind the arras of the chamber, the curtain of the hall, or the rood screen of the church? Those who gleefully murmur to this sickened world how I, the so-called crouchback, killed Henry of Lancaster, my own brothers George of Clarence and Edward the King, and, now I am on my throne, swim deeper in the innocent blood of my nephews?' Richard laughed mirthlessly as if savouring some secret jest. Then he rose, kicked at one of the logs stacked to the side of the great canopied hearth. 'It's a lie, Francis. You lie. Your eyes lie. In God's name, they all lie and you will be the person who sticks such lies in their throats!' He raised his head and stared at me, biting his lower lip, all the time playing with a dagger, a small bejewelled affair, stuck in a small gold-encrusted scabbard in his belt, Richard's favourite gesture when he was angry or nervous. 'You are to London, Francis. You are to go there and find the truth of this. The whereabouts of my nephews.' He glared viciously at me as if fighting some private inner demon.

'You will have your letters and your warrants to search out the truth. If Brackenbury is guilty, I will have his head. His or any others, be it the highest in the land, even if it is Buckingham. He will hang from the stars of heaven!' I stared coolly back. Buckingham, haughty Buckingham with his dark-red hair and his arrogant hawklike face, always dressed in purple, always hinting how he, too, had royal blood in his veins. Henry Stafford, second Duke of Buckingham, was a man to watch. Richard and I stared at each other. Buckingham had helped Richard to the throne, sworn great oaths and made sweet promises, but Richard watched him, always on guard. The Duke had not followed our progress through the kingdom after Richard's coronation. Instead, making excuses with kind words and honeyed phrases, he had hurried back to Brecon and his powerful fiefdom in the south-west.

Richard did not trust him. I did not like him. Had not the King given into Buckingham's hands Bishop John Morton, that arch-plotter, that man of the church who hid a voracious hunger for temporal power? Morton, Henry Tudor's greatest supporter in England. Richard and I had wanted Morton held fast in the Tower, but Buckingham with his sly ways and devious talk had persuaded the King to release Morton into his care. Worse, only two days previously Richard and I had listened to spies from Buckingham's household. How the Duke was plotting mischief, conspiring with the

King's enemies. He was deep in conversation with that sanctimonious bitch, Margaret Beaufort, the Countess of Richmond and mother of Henry Tudor, a woman only allowed her liberty because of her second marriage to the powerful Lord Stanley.

Richard broke the silence, smiling secretively at me.

'Even if it's Buckingham,' he whispered, 'I will have his head! You are to leave no stone unturned, encounter no obstacle!' Richard looked at me, touching me gently on the cheek before he stalked out of the hall, shouting for his grooms, huntsmen. He wanted to hunt and forget his cares. I just sat in that cold hall. Anne came down. Warm, sleepy-eyed. She clutched my hand and pressed her body against mine but I ignored her, so, wrapped in her heavy cloak, she went into the buttery at the far end of the hall to organise the servants. I watched her go, envying her absorption with ordinary daily tasks while I wondered if I had fastened my fortunes, and those of Anne, to a falling star? Bright and fiery but falling like Lucifer through the heavens. Richard Plantagenet, fourth son of Richard of York, the brother and uncle of kings, now wearing the crown himself. I tried to be cold, impassive, logical, forgetting the young boy I had grown up with, united by those deep bonds forged in childhood. But, who else could I follow? Two young boys, his brother's sons, supposedly locked away in the Tower of London? Or the red dragon, Henry Tudor, the Welshman, now skulking in the chill bleak courts of Brittany? No, I was held fast to Richard of York.

But were the stories true? Was Richard a murderous assassin? Did he have the same cunning and lust for killing as the White Boar, his favourite emblem? Was Richard my master, now my King, the boy who had played in the dusty courtyards and reedy marshes of Middleham, a regicide? This prince, who founded chantries, loved music and learning, a bloodstained sinner in God's eyes? The man who had knighted me on our campaigns against the Scots; created me a Viscount, Constable of Wallingford Castle, Chief Butler and Chamberlain of his household. Was he really a murderer? Only weeks earlier I had encouraged him to take the marble chair of King's Bench, the symbol of royal justice in Westminster Hall. I had been there carrying the sword of state when Richard and his frail Queen, Anne, walked the broad ribbon of red cloth up to the high altar of the Abbey to be crowned with all the pomp and glory of church and state as Richard III of England.

Richard was my king, but, on that morning, I had to face the rumours and scandals I had so far ignored. His brother had died: Edward, King of England, golden-haired, standing over six feet, the champion of England, the destroyer of the House of Lancaster. He had seized the throne and held it fast, marrying the woman who caught his heart and satisfied his every lust, Elizabeth Woodville, a widow and, as some men said, a sorceress. On her he had fathered many children, promising the crown to his eldest son, Edward, but then the King died. Suddenly, in the midst of his pleasure, whilst boating on the Thames; and the eagles had gathered. Richard proclaimed himself as Protector, whispering fiercely to me how he would have to defend himself against the Woodvilles. They would have him arrested and secretly done to death as they had Clarence who dared to conspire and whisper against the Queen. Richard never forgot Clarence, nor did he forget the whispers. He remembered them. Oh, yes. One in particular, brought to him by Bishop Stillington of Bath and Wells. A curious story. How Edward IV's marriage to the Woodville was null and void for Edward had already been betrothed to the Lady Eleanor Butler. If this was so, and I could imagine Buckingham with the silver whispering and golden arguments, Edward IV's two sons were bastards. They were illegitimate stock and could never wear the crown of England. Richard had believed this. He proclaimed his brother's marriage bigamous, seizing the two princes, locking them in the Tower and taking the crown himself.

There was no other way. True or false, what did it matter? If Richard had not become King, sooner or later the Woodvilles, because of their hold over the young princes, would have destroyed him. What man wants to live his life in the shadow of the axe or the nightmare of dreadful death in some secret dungeon? But murder? Infanticide? I knew Richard well. A man of sharp contrasts. On his orders the Bishop of London had forced Mistress Jane Shore, his brother's paramour, to walk through the streets of London dressed only in her shift, carrying a candle, as public atonement for her fleshly desires. Yet Richard was no stranger to such lusts. He himself had a bastard son, the Lord John, and at least one other illegitimate offspring. He was a master actor, cautious and subtle, able to mask his true feelings behind conceits and stratagems. When Lord Hastings fell, Richard had staged a masque as cunning as anything devised on some town stage. A hot, sweaty summer day in the council chamber in the Tower; Richard, pulling back his jerkin sleeve showing his arm, thinner, more emaciated than the other, a defect from birth. Richard, however, accused Hastings of withering it by witchcraft, saying he would not dine until the traitor had lost his head. In a few violent bloody minutes Richard had Hastings executed and others of his coven, Morton and Rotherham of York, placed in custody.

There had been other guises, other conceits: Buckingham offering him the crown at Baynards Castle and Richard reluctantly accepting it. Oh, I had seen it all. Now, was this Richard play-acting again? The role of the anxious uncle, when he knew full well the true fate of his nephews? I rose and began shouting for servants to prepare for my departure. Secretly, in my heart, I swore an oath: if Richard had slain his nephews and dragged me into some deadly masque, I would leave him and flee beyond the seas.

TWO

Two days it took, two days of frenetic packing of trunks, chests and coffers. After a secret council with the King, I made to leave Minster Lovell, accompanied by six retainers and my faithful steward, Thomas Belknap. Ah, Belknap, a great scurrier and spy. An able clerk, a former priest who had been dismissed by Bishop Morton from his prebend in Ely. A secretive man, Belknap; he burned with a lasting hatred, or so he said, against his former bishop and anything to do with the House of Lancaster. He and I left the courtyard of Minster Lovell on a cool, clear summer morning. Behind me stood Anne, in a sea-blue dress fringed with gold, her black hair unveiled, falling down around her sweet face like some cloying mist. Above her, staring out of the window of the solar, King Richard watched me impassively, his hand half raised. His sombre stare troubled me as we made our way along the rutted tracks, dried hard by the sun, before reaching the old Roman road south to London.

We entered the city by the north gate, skirting Smithfield and the stinking messes around Newgate. They say London is a wondrous city but I could see why Richard hated the place; it made me homesick for the green softness of Minster Lovell. The narrow streets were piled high with refuse which hordes of kites and ravens plundered alongside wandering dogs and naked, filthy children. All was dark, the light being blocked out by the leaning gables and gilt-edged storeys of the narrow houses huddled together as if conspiring to keep out God's sun. Slowly we made our way through the noisy throng of Cheapside and its concourse of merchants, men whom Richard distrusted. They served their coffers and their purses, eager to obey a crowned ape if he guaranteed their profits. Such men failed us. They were only interested in their robes of velvet and brocade, their blue satin hats turned up at the brim, or their doublets of blue and green. More eager that their shoulders should be padded or the sleeves slashed with silk than for the politics of the realm. Ah, well! I shall not see them again! Time-servers all!

Eventually we reached Bishopsgate, entering the main courtyard of Crosby Hall, whose roofs towered higher than any other London dwelling. Richard had hired it as his London home.

Before I left Minster Lovell, he had given me warrants and letters allowing me the use of the chambers and stables, and purveyance. The courtyard was full of masons, carpenters and other workmen. Richard wanted the building extended even further, commissioning no less a person than John Howard, newly created Duke of Norfolk, as surveyor of the works. I was to meet Howard there and take secret council with him over what Richard had told me. However, the Duke was absent and I had to rest content with the jumbled messages of a pompous steward about how and when the Duke would return.

Leaving Belknap to look after the horses and see to our trunks and caskets, I made my way up to a chamber. I would have liked to have slept but the King had emphasised the urgency of the task entrusted to me, so I refreshed myself with watered ale and sweetmeats, washing the dust from my face with sweet petal-water as I considered what I should do next. I decided on secrecy and left Crosby Hall only with Belknap, instructing him not to display my emblem or livery. As Richard's chamberlain, I was well-known in the city and people would whisper about my secret return. Moreover, the King had his enemies, agents of Henry Tudor and other silent malignants, only too pleased to strike at Richard's trusted friend and counsellor, or so I thought myself.

I made my way down to the river, planning to travel to Westminster along the dark sweeping curve of the Thames. Belknap hired a boat and soon we were mid-stream. We rowed through the fast currents which roared past the white pillars of London Bridge, still blackened by the attack of the Bastard of Fauconberg, in those heady days when the House of York still struggled to survive. Around us other wherry boats scurried across the water like flies over a village pond. Belknap told the boatman to keep away from the gorgeous bannered barges of the merchants and other nobles, men who might well recognise me.

At last we came in sight of Westminster Palace, sheltering under the lee of the great abbey. A welcoming sight. The gables, towers, battlements, steep roofs and arched windows of its buildings swept down towards the waterside. The boatman pulled in towards the shore, close to the palace wall which was protected by dense thickets and bushes. We rowed past the King's stairs near the main wharf, landing at the Abbot's Steps and making our way stealthily up to the palace. We ignored the clerks, officials, receivers and sheriffs' men, using the tumult and shouts of the pastrycooks who always throng there to slip quietly into the great hall. I left Belknap staring up at its beautiful wooden roof supported by sprung beams borne on the backs of angels, so exquisitely carved they seemed in flight. My head down, concealed by a hood, I pushed my way through courtiers, servants, red-capped judges and lawyers who, despite the heat, still wore their skullcaps and gold-fringed robes. I was the King's Chamberlain; many who worked there, whether they be servants, stable-boys or singing children from the royal chapel of St. Stephen, were really under my jurisdiction. I approached a steward and, swearing him to secrecy, made him take me through winding passages and up flights of stairs to the office of the Star Chamber where John Russell, Richard's Chancellor and Bishop of Lincoln, kept state.

I was ushered in through a side door and walked across, my boots rapping noisily on the lozenge-shaped black and white tiles, so smooth and polished you felt you were walking across a mirror. Around me the deep, blue-coated walls were covered with small gold stars which gave the room its name. Russell, a diminutive figure, sat enthroned in a high-backed chair, swathed in costly purple and gold robes. All around him, their table-tops littered with parchment, wax, pens and inkpots, sat perspiring clerks, each working on some letter or document the Chancellor wished despatched. The Bishop looked up as I entered but continued dictating quietly to a clerk until finished. He clapped his hands softly and murmured something; the clerks immediately smiled, rose and hurriedly left. Once the room was empty, Russell waved me to a chair beside him.

'Lord Lovell,' he murmured, not even bothering to stir himself. 'You are most welcome. I did not know you were coming.'

'In haste,' I replied. 'His Grace is still in Oxfordshire and despatched me immediately.'

'His Grace is well?' The small, pebble-black eyes scrutinised me.

'His Grace is well,' I answered, noticing the slight flicker of Russell's small, pursed lips. I did not like the Bishop, nor he me. He did not serve Richard well, but what does that matter now? We were not served well and we paid for our stupidity. Nevertheless, I respected Russell and observed the civilities. After all, on that hot summer afternoon we both knew why I was in London. I leaned across the table and handed him a small scroll.

'His Grace has sent you this,' I said. Russell looked at it before placing it unopened to one side.

'I know what it says,' he smiled. 'And so do you!'

'The Princes?'

Russell coughed, dry, like the lawyer he was, preparing to make a speech.

'You mean the illegitimate issue of King Edward IV?'

'I mean the Princes,' I said. 'Where are they?'

The Bishop spread thin, skeletal, vein-rimmed hands.

'How do I know? They were in the royal apartments in the Tower and were then moved.' He looked up at the wooden carved ceiling. 'Yes,' he continued. 'A few weeks after the King's coronation, first to the Garden Tower and then to the upper storey of the White Tower. After that ...' His dry voice trailed off. He looked away as if studying the colour-glazed windows of the room.

'You have been to the Tower?' I asked accusingly.

'No.'

'So, how do you know?'

'Sir Robert Brackenbury came to see me.'

'What did he say?'

'Very little. The fellow was agitated. He said the Princes were gone,' Russell replied.

'When was this?'

Russell bit his lower lip.

'Brackenbury came about five days ago. The morning of August 2nd.'

'Did you question him about the details?'

'A little. I asked him when he had last checked on his prisoners. He replied the week previously.'

'A week previously?' I shouted.

Russell grinned mirthlessly.

'I said the same.'

'Did you immediately order a search?'

Russell glared at me.

'That is not my responsibility, Lord Lovell. I cannot act on this matter without His Grace's express command.' He leaned across the table, steepling his fingers. 'The Princes are gone,' he explained patiently. 'The King is only a few weeks crowned. Around us men plot in covens, conspiracies and confederations, secret meetings at the dead of night. For God's sake, Lovell, what am I to do? Say the Princes are gone and so fan the hopes of these malignants? Or worse, if people think they are dead.' Russell let his hands drop. 'Their father, King Edward IV, was much loved and so were the young princes. Many thought they were sweet and beautiful children.' Russell stopped speaking and looked away. 'The younger one,' he continued softly, 'the Duke of York, was joyous and witty, nimble and ever ready for dances and games.'

My heart went cold. Here was Richard's own Chancellor, a leading bishop of the realm, and I could read his mind. He thought the Princes were dead, perhaps murdered on Richard's orders, and that I was part of this horrible travesty.

'My Lord Bishop!'

Russell stared at me under his eyebrows.

'My Lord Bishop, I swear on the gospels, on my soul, I know nothing of this and neither does the King!'

'But what about those around him?' he asked. 'The henchmen, Sir James Tyrrell, William Catesby, Richard Ratcliffe? It would not be the first time that the servants of a Prince have tried to anticipate his every wish!'

I glared back. What was Russell referring to? Thomas à Beckett? Or events nearer home? Men did claim Richard had a hand in the murder of Henry of Lancaster, even in the death of his brother, George of Clarence. Once again the suspicion flitted across my mind like a bat through the darkness. Was this all a sham? Did Richard know the truth? Were Russell's suspicions the real truth? Just because we serve princes it does not mean we know their minds.

'Is that all you know, my Lord?'

Russell toyed with the gold-fringed tassel of his robe.

'Yes, Lovell, that is all I know,' he replied.

'And those plots, conspiracies?' I asked, reasserting myself.

'The King knows. I have sent letters north.' Russell fished amongst the leaves of parchment strewn across his desk and pulled out a small ivory-white roll bound by a scarlet cord.

'A copy of a letter,' he muttered. 'From one of our spies. You may read it. Take it with you.'

Tired of Russell's guarded looks and secretive talk, I snatched the parchment, rose and walked back towards the door.

'Lovell!' the Bishop called out. I ignored him but he called again. 'If the Princes are dead,' the Bishop said, 'then so are we. The King should watch himself. Be on guard, for the deaths or disappearance of those two boys could bring him and all about him crashing down.' I stared coolly back but the Bishop was unflinching. 'I mean all of us, Lovell. It is a wise man who looks to the future.' The Bishop smiled. 'Of course, my Lord, if you repeat what I have just said, I will stoutly deny it. I am a loyal servant of King Richard.' I nodded and left, Russell's dire warning and his guarded comments ringing in my ears.

Three

I went back to the main hall and collected a still gawking Belknap before returning to Crosby Place. The workmen had all gone, there was no sign of Howard, and my retainers had ensconced themselves in comfortable quarters. I interrupted their evening drinking and dicing to send a message to Sir Robert Brackenbury at the Tower commanding him to wait for me on the morrow. I roused the steward of the kitchen to prepare cold meats, wine and a dish of fruit and a disgruntled servant laid the meal out in the hall. Belknap sat opposite me, silent, absorbed, so I thought, in his own private world of bitter vengeance. I unrolled the report Russell had given me. I have it now, along with all my papers. They left those for me. Strange, I never thought I would re-read it in such circumstances.

'Know you' (it began, leaving out the usual courtesies) 'that I have travelled from the eastern shires as far west as the Severn and have met many men who now conspire against His Grace. They call him a wretched, bloody and usurping boar. They gather in secret covens and sworn confederacies to plot the King's downfall. They accuse him of usurping the throne and ill-using his nephews. Men say, know you, how the aforesaid Princes are dead, killed secretly by their usurper, their bodies flung into th Thames. Others say the boys are beyond the seas but if they are not, and have met a grievous death, these men say they will change their

29

coats and accept Henry Tudor from Brittany. Know
you, how men say that the Queen Elizabeth Woodville
has sent many secret messages, pledges, and even
plenteous gold to the Tudor. Worst still, she has
pledged her own daughter in marriage to the
Welshman to effect a union between the houses of York
and Lancaster. They also say my Lord of Buckingham's
heart has turned against the King; indeed, he is sending
secret messages to his tenants, retainers and servants in
Kent. Cursors are constantly despatched between him
and Lord Stanley's wife, the Lady Margaret Beaufort.
Men say the Tudor will come in late autumn and our
Lord the King would best be prepared for his landing.

'Know you that the King's spies and agents in these
shires, towns and villages are daily threatened if their
allegiance to His Grace is discovered. My Lord of
Buckingham has one agent, a person named Percivalle,
who has greatly vexed them. A body squire of the royal
household, Edmund Waters, whom I was supposed to
meet in Colchester, has been found dead. The coroner
ruled his death was murder by person or persons
unknown. Men say he was attacked by outlaws but I
believe he was executed by either Percivalle or others
from my Lord Buckingham's retinue.

'The men in this conspiracy are ...'

The spy listed, amongst others, Sir Thomas Browne
of Surrey, Sir John Fogge of Kent (he whom Richard
had taken personally by the hand to pledge his loyalty),
the Courtneys from Devon, the Woodvilles and Sir
William Haute of Kent. The list was lengthy and,
despite the warmth, I shivered as I read it. These
conspirators were not hotheads, men who had nothing
to lose. Many I knew personally and respected; they had
been friends and confidants of King Edward IV.
Middle-aged, wealthy men, able to command the
allegiance of their servants and the respect of others,
serving in both Parliament and the royal household.

Their allegiance to the House of York had been unswerving and unquestioning. So why this conspiracy? Who or what had changed their hearts, as well as that of my Lord of Buckingham? Richard's seizure of the throne? True, even I had wavered when I had heard about it, but better Richard any day than the Woodville pack or the kingdom ruled by some pretty boy who would not hold his own. After all, Edward IV had done no worse; he had displaced Henry VI of Lancaster and killed Henry's young son in that bloody fight around Tewkesbury Abbey.

I thought of Russell, a man skilled in church and state yet his allegiance was now wavering. Above all, Buckingham. He who had supported Richard throughout. He was party to the seizure of the Princes; now he had changed, while his sinister agent, Percivalle, was busy as any farmer sowing seeds of discontent. The Princes must be dead; their murder had changed mens' hearts and the King was tricking me. No, I lie. At that time, sitting in the shadows of the wood-panelled hall of Crosby Place, I believed the Princes were gone and half suspected Richard was their bloody abductor.

I dismissed Belknap, sitting opposite me, his goblet half raised to his lips, watching me strangely. After a while I adjourned to my own chamber. I had bloody dreams that night, dreadful phantasms, horrid nightmares of being in an upper chamber in the Tower. I knew it was there, for through an open casement window I could hear the caw of the ravens and sounds from the river. Two young boys asleep on pallet beds. Above them, a shadowy figure, dagger in hand; in the other hand a soft, thick, velvet cushion which would block your mouth, cutting the breath off for ever. Time and again I called out for him to stop. Each time he turned I saw Richard's face, pale, white, pinched, the green eyes staring malevolently at me, his red hair flaring out like the wings of a hawk as it closes in for the kill. God knows, I tossed and turned, wrestling with my fears. I was finally roused just after dawn by a servant, my eyes still heavy with sleep, my throat dry, my body covered in a sheen of sweat.

The fellow declared that His Grace the Duke of Norfolk had arrived and was waiting for me below stairs in the buttery. I wrapped a cloak about me and, bellowing for Belknap, hurried down. I knew Norfolk well and liked him; God rest his soul and forgive the evil he did but, after such a night, I welcomed his arrival fondly, remembering this bustling, self-important man who enjoyed playing cards and chess and delighted in nothing better than a mummer's play, or listening to skilled musicians. He was nonetheless a brave soldier, a shrewd general and one of the best sea captains England ever had. God bless the Jockey of Norfolk!

The Duke was waiting for me in the buttery. He was dressed in a long gown of black satin lined with purple velvet over a satin doublet of a popinjay colour with hose to match, feet thrust into stout leather riding-boots. His thick, fat fingers were covered with rings, a collar of gold with roses and suns on a chain of black silk with a hanger of gold around his neck. He looked an incongruous sight. A mixture of yeoman and courtier, soldier and scholar, his huge frame seemed to fill the small room. In one hand he held a deep-bowled goblet of wine, in the other, some food snatched from the kitchen. He stood, like the sailor he was, legs apart as if commanding a cog against French or Scottish corsairs. His white leonine head was thrown back, his fleshy face wreathed in smiles, though his eyes were hard and watchful.

'Lovell!' he roared, putting the goblet on the table and tossing the food into a corner. Wiping his hands and mouth on his robe, he swept me up in one great bear hug so I could smell his sweat and perfume, as well as the gusts of wine-soaked breath as he kissed me hard on each cheek.

'Be careful!' he whispered. 'Be very careful what you say! Belknap is behind you. Get rid of him!' I smiled, stepped away and turned round. The Duke was right, Belknap lounged against the door; dressed completely in dark velvet, he looked like some bird of prey.

'Thomas,' I said softly. 'Leave us for the moment.' The man nodded and walked away. Norfolk, going after him, closed the door and this small gesture stirred my fears. When the Duke turned, his face was grim. We sat like two servant boys on stools facing each other.

'His Grace has sent you,' Norfolk began. I was about to stammer some polite reply but Norfolk clutched me tightly by the knee.

'Francis, no lies! I have heard the rumours: in Cheapside, near the Standard, around St. Paul's, in the villages and towns of Kent, men say the Princes have gone, been killed. They talk of conspiracy and rebellion.'

'What if such rumours are true?'

Norfolk turned and spat in the corner.

'God's teeth, man. What do I care about two puking bastards? Are we to sit on the ground and mourn for them? You have been in battle, Lovell. You were in Scotland with me when we were chasing King James's bare-arsed soldiers across the heather. We took towns and sacked them. Young boys died then. Who weeps for them? Or the young Desmond boys?' The Duke looked at me. 'You remember the Irish earl. He told King Edward that he could have married better and the Woodville bitch never forgave him. She later had him killed and his young bairns with him.' The Duke tossed his head. 'I do not care for the Princes. I care for myself, Lovell. I am almost sixty years of age. I have been fighting for the House of York for almost a quarter of a century. I joined young Edward at the battle of Towton with a sword in one hand and a bag of gold in the other. Since then I have not looked back. I owe all to the

House of York.' He stopped and stared at the ground.
'The fate of the Princes,' he continued quietly,
'wherever they may be, heaven or hell, Ireland or
France, is only important if men can prove that they
were killed by their uncle. That is what bothers me. The
growing whispering campaign against our King.
Everywhere I go I hear the same stories. How the King
is a monster, born with hair and teeth, a crouchback. A
hog. The despoiler of children. These rumours have
been carefully sown and this business of the Princes
might well be the fiery torch to the dry stubble.'

'You have heard of Percivalle?' I asked.

'Yes, I have.' The Duke snorted with laughter. 'And if
I catch him, I will hang him as high as the spire of St.
Paul's!'

'And my Lord of Buckingham?' I asked curiously.

'My Lord of Buckingham is a popinjay. Who knows?'
The Duke pursed his lips.

'Who knows what?'

'Buckingham claims he has royal blood, claiming
descent from Edward III's son, Edmund of Woodstock.
He has even the right to bear his arms. He is also kin to
the Beauforts and they have never been friends of the
House of York.'

'Do you think Buckingham aims so high?'

Norfolk shrugged. 'Perhaps he sees himself as
kingmaker. God knows.'

'And the Princes?'

Norfolk grasped both my hands in his. 'I know
nothing of them but I tell you, Francis, for the love of
the sweet God, the only way to stop these rumours is to
find the Princes and produce them alive and well.'

I decided to grasp the nettle firmly.

'Have you visited Brackenbury in the Tower?'

Norfolk shook his head and gave the same answer as
Russell. On this matter he dare not speak without the
King's special permission.

'Do you think,' I said slowly, 'that His Grace would have the boys murdered?' I saw the anger flare in the old man's eyes. 'I am,' I continued smoothly, 'as close a friend to the King as you are.'

Norfolk smiled.

'I do not think Richard has killed the Princes,' he answered. 'Why should he? If he had wanted them to disappear why not move them to some forlorn castle, as happened to their forebears, Edward II and Richard II? No, I do not think the King killed them and I know Sir Robert Brackenbury too well. He would not have innocent blood on his hands.'

'I am to see Brackenbury later.'

'Good,' Norfolk replied. 'And now these conspiracies?'

Our conversation turned to what Norfolk had learnt, which reflected the same warnings I had gathered from Russell's spy: the southern counties, particularly Kent and Devon, were seething hotbeds of conspiracy. Norfolk announced what preparations he was making, declining to move against Buckingham until he had positive proof. After that he left as abruptly as he came.

I poured some wine, calling Belknap into the buttery to join me.

'My Duke of Norfolk,' Belknap commented, 'seems not to like me.'

'My Duke of Norfolk,' I mimicked in reply, 'likes nobody but himself. He has risen fast,' I continued. 'Richard's premier general and duke, the recipient of our King's lavish generosity.'

'He was also,' Belknap drily interrupted, 'until recently one of those who had access to the Tower. If the young Duke of York is dead, as rumour has it, then my Lord the Duke will benefit.'

'What do you mean?'

Belknap turned, making sure the door was closed.

'I mean, my Lord, that before we left Minster Lovell,

you told me the general lines of this business. Like any good dog, I keep my ear to the ground. The city and the palace abound with rumours of how the Princes may be gone. Perhaps dead. I am right, am I not?'

'Yes, Belknap, you are correct. But what has that to do with Howard?'

'Three things. First, until July 17th past my Lord of Norfolk had access to the Tower. Secondly, he gave his word when the young Duke of York was handed over by Elizabeth Woodville on June 20th last, that no harm would come to the boy. Finally, the young duke was married to the Mowbray heiress. The duke has always claimed that inheritance.'

I stared at Belknap, that most knowledgeable of men.

'If you are a good dog, Belknap, then still keep your ear hard to the ground.' I went closer to him. 'I would be gratified if you could pursue this matter yourself by stealth and secrecy.'

Four

Once Belknap had left, I hurriedly dressed and, cloaked and hooded, made my way back to the riverside where I hired a skiff to take me upstream to the Tower. It was still early morning and a thick mist hung over the river, sealing it in silence and obscuring the buildings along the banks. Despite its reputation as a palace, a royal menagerie and treasury of the Crown, I always found the Tower a bleak, lonely place. On that morning, with the fog swirling round as I disembarked on the gravel quayside, I found it as sombre as ever, the huge, yellow-beaked ravens greeting my arrival with their raucous cawing as I made my way up into the entrance. An officer wearing the royal livery greeted me.

There were the usual interminable questions and checks from the guards as we entered the darkness of the gateways which controlled the entrances to the concentric ring of towers.

Eventually we came to the royal apartments. Brackenbury was waiting, ushering me into a luxurious, spacious room, with clean rushes on the floor. I remember it well with its blood-red drapes, huge bed covered by a blue and gold canopy and the chests stacked high, some open, spilling out clothes, belts, hose and other apparel. A stark contrast to the buildings I had just passed through.

Sir Robert Brackenbury was small, stout, deep-chested, with huge, long arms which made him an excellent swordsman. His face was swarthy, bearded, his dark hair hung in ringlets which he constantly wore gathered behind his head. He was a northerner, born near Baynards Castle, and had served as Richard's treasurer. On any other occasion we would have greeted each other most civilly for we were on friendly if not cordial terms. On that particular morning, however, he greeted me as an enemy. He dismissed the officer, showing me to a chair. He did not bother to offer a goblet of wine or the tray of pastry doucettes I saw standing on the table.

'I received your message, Lord Lovall.' His voice was curt, betraying a northern burr.

I waited until he had sat down, and leaned across.

'Sir Robert, we have known each other what, eight, ten years?' He stared unblinkingly back. 'Sir Robert,' I persisted, 'I am not an inquisitor. The King has received your news.' I shrugged. 'Naturally, there are questions to ask.'

'Naturally,' Brackenbury sardonically replied. 'But it is the answers which I find hard.'

'Sir Robert,' I began, realising that any attempt at tact or diplomacy was proving fruitless. 'You were appointed as Constable on 17 July last?'

'Yes, I was.'

'You took up office immediately?'

'I did.'

'And you checked on your charges, the young Princes?'

'The bastard lords, Edward and Richard?' Brackenbury was quick to reply. 'Yes, twice,' he continued. 'The Princes were in the Garden Tower overlooking the river. The King had instructed me, for reasons of security, to remove them deeper into the Tower and to stop them playing in the gardens.'

'Why was that?'

'There were rumours of plans to free the Princes. An

attack from the riverside would have been easy to achieve. They would not be the first captives to escape from the Tower.'

'And where were they moved to?'

'To one of the turrets in the White Tower.'

I thought quickly about what I knew of the fortress. Brackenbury's answer made sense. The White Tower was a huge donjon; it could only be stormed once the rest of the Tower had been taken. There were two floors, the upper containing the Chapel of St. John and other royal offices, but there were chambers in each of the four turrets.

'You checked the Princes? When again?'

'About two weeks later. I did my formal round tour of the Tower. I went to the Princes' chamber but it was deserted.' Brackenbury stopped speaking and chewed his lower lip. 'No gaoler, no boys. Nothing seemed touched. Clothing, bolsters, blankets. Nothing was missing except a set of garments for each of the boys.'

'And the previous time?'

'You mean the second time I saw them?'

'How were the children? You saw them?'

'They seemed well enough. Happy enough—in the circumstances.'

'What do you mean?'

Sir Robert positively squirmed in his chair, his face paler, a fine sheen of sweat on his brow.

'In the circumstances,' he said bleakly. 'For God's sake, man, they were mere bairns. They missed their mother, their sisters. They were frightened.'

'Of what?'

'Of what might happen to them.' Brackenbury heaved a sigh. 'That is why I kept my visits so rare. They were secure enough. I could not help them. I am a soldier, not a gaoler. I excused myself under the pretence that there was more in the Tower than just two princes who were well looked after.' Sir Robert paused and wiped his brow with the cuff of his jerkin before continuing. 'I hated visiting them.'

'They were kept well?'

'Of course. They wanted for nothing.'

'Except their freedom?'

'Except their freedom,' Brackenbury snapped back. 'But I was under orders.' He leaned forward. 'Remember, Lovell, we both serve the King. It was Richard who ordered his nephews kept close.'

'Their servants?' I said coolly, ignoring his distress.

'Once they had been moved from the Garden Tower, before I became Constable, their servants were dismissed?'

'So who looked after them?'

'A varlet named William Slaughter.'

'Who was he?'

'I do not know. I simply received instructions from the King that all their servants were dismissed except for Slaughter, or Black Will as he was commonly called.'

'An ominous name.'

'Oh, he was friendly enough. A young man, in about his twentieth summer. Small, rather plump, sandy-haired and cheery-faced. His appearance belied his name.'

'So why the Black?'

'He constantly wore black clothing. An affectation, but the young princes seemed to like him well enough.'

'Was Slaughter from the Tower garrison?'

'No,' Brackenbury replied. He rose and wiped his face with a damp towel. Only then did he pour me a goblet of wine, thick, red and heady. I sipped it gratefully, allowing Brackenbury some respite from my constant questioning.

'Slaughter,' Brackenbury continued, 'was from one of the household retinues.'

'Whose?' I asked. 'The King's? Buckingham's?'

Brackenbury rose again and went to a small leather

coffer, one of many stacked against the far wall. He opened it, pulled out a roll of vellum which he unfolded and studied for a while.

'No,' he replied slowly. 'From the accounts of the Treasurer here, Slaughter had been in the retinue of the Duke of Norfolk.' Brackenbury clicked his fingers. 'Yes, he was Howard's man. I remember the children used to mimic his countrified tongue and strange accent.' Brackenbury shrugged. 'But Slaughter, too, has disappeared.'

I sipped again from the wine-cup. Brackenbury was obviously agitated. Indeed, up to his violent death he remained a distressed, anxious man, wrestling with his own nightmares. Now I only wished he had been truthful then and not left it too late. Perhaps something could have been done. Yet, he was a brave swordsman. He was one of the last to die. God save his soul!

On that mist-laden morning, however, neither of us had a glimpse of the future, even though what we were discussing would be the harbinger of all our fates. I remember asking Brackenbury about any visitors seeing the young boys.

'Only two,' Brackenbury replied. 'The first was the Duke of Norfolk, shortly after the coronation. He came to see the Duke of York.'

'You attended the meeting?' I asked.

'No,' he replied. 'It was before I took up office.'

'And the second visitor?'

'The Duke of Buckingham,' Brackenbury snapped, making no attempt to disguise his contempt for the man.

'When did he come?'

'The day before my last visit,' Brackenbury replied. 'He arrived with a massive concourse of retainers, claiming he was preparing to leave London to meet His Grace at Gloucester. I remember objecting to the large numbers of retainers in the Tower. They drew on our supplies and, with their wandering about, hampered my guardianship.'

'Did Buckingham see the Princes alone?

Brackenbury smiled thinly.

'No. He wanted to, but I insisted that Slaughter be present. His conversation with the two princes was nothing but ordinary chitter-chatter. After that, he left the Tower. I was glad to see him gone.'

'Slaughter,' I said. 'Did you see him after that?'

'No, I did not. He was espied on the day after Buckingham left but, after that, he disappeared like some will-o'-the-wisp. I have searched for him,' Brackenbury concluded, 'as I have for the two princes, sending my best scurriers and most discreet spies to the main ports. I have also taken careful scrutiny of what is happening in the city. There is no sign or trace of any of them.'

'Has the castle garrison noticed anything amiss?'

'Nothing.' Brackenbury heaved a sigh. 'Some of them do not even know the Princes are gone.' I extended my cup and Brackenbury slopped more wine into it.

'Sir Robert,' I said. 'Has any other member of the King's household besides myself, henchmen such as Catesby, Ratcliffe or Tyrrell, visited the Tower?'

Brackenbury's eyes slid away.

'Sir James Tyrrell,' he replied softly. 'The King's Master of Horse. He came just before I found the boys had disappeared. But he never saw them or approached their apartments. He only came to draw stores for the King's progress in the north. Buckingham was the last. It was only after he left that I checked on them and found them gone.'

'And what then?' I asked.

'I have told you. I immediately ordered searches and sent my fastest scurrier north with a letter for the King.'

'Then there is nothing else?'

'Nothing,' Brackenbury replied. 'There were groups

of men who used to assemble on the far bank. I had them watched but they were not a menace, only bully boys and felons from the city alleyways. About three days ago such groups disappeared.'

'My Duke of Buckingham?' I asked.

'He has not returned nor made any attempt to communicate with me or anyone within the Tower.' I nodded and studied the intricate design on the Persian carpet Brackenbury had laid down in his chamber. The shadow of an idea was beginning to form. Brackenbury was nervous, agitated. He was hiding something, concealing something terrible. But at the same time I sensed the man was innocent. Brackenbury was what he died, a faithful soldier, ready to carry out to the death any order issued by the King. I only wish he had told me the truth. Perhaps greater evil might have been avoided.

After a few more desultory remarks Brackenbury agreed to show me the chamber where the two princes had been kept. We left the royal apartments and crossed a small green, the place where Lord William Hastings had his head shorn off for conspiring to free the same princes whose disappearance had brought me to the Tower. The entire area was dominated by the huge donjon or White Tower. We climbed up some outside stairs into the Chapel of St. John, one of the most beautiful churches in Christendom. The walls were covered with beautiful murals, done in gold and vermilion. The floor tiles, glazed white, bore crosses and leopards couchant while every window was filled with multi-coloured glass so the entire room seemed to swim in a sea of gorgeous colour. A stark contrast to the grey, bleak, staircase chamber above.

The cell of the bastard princes was spacious but stark, despite pathetic attempts to enliven it with tawdry hangings. There was a large trestle bed, covered in heavy, white, gold-fringed bolsters on a feather-bed mattress half covered with blankets and a tapestry canopy. A large cupboard stood near the wall. I opened it. Musty clothes were piled high: a small jerkin, hose, a few robes and battered boots. The two tables were covered with caskets, scraps of parchment, a pen and an inkhorn. Most pathetic of all, the young princes' toys: two small bows, quivers half-full of arrows, a wooden horse, some beads and a rusty dagger snapped at the hilt. The windows were no more than arrow-slits which overlooked the water-meadows of the Thames. The room was sombre, filled by a dreadful, baleful silence which not even the cawing of the rooks shattered. Just silence. Brooding, heavy, oppressive. There were no trap-doors, no other entrances. Brackenbury had every right to claim the Princes could not have escaped or been abducted. They would have to cross the chapel, skirt chambers, pass by sentries and go through at least three doors just to reach the Tower green. Even if they had reached there, any of the guards encircling the towers or walls would have espied them.

I heard Brackenbury stir behind me. He was as uncomfortable as I was.

'Sir Robert?' I asked. 'On the sacrament, are you in any way responsible for the Princes' disappearance?'

'No!' His honest face was taut and anxious but in my heart I felt he was lying.

Five

I next saw the royal physician, Sir Giles Argentine, a graduate of Strasburg, who had served in the household of Edward IV. I met him in his own chambers in the Garden Tower. Tall, completely bald, an ascetic with sharp eyes and a narrow, hatchet-like face, he was dressed soberly in fustian brown, the only luxury being a small ring on one of his long, bony fingers and a simple gold chain round his neck. I mention these details for most doctors are open to bribes but Argentine struck me as an honest man. He invited me in and poured two goblets of chilled white Rhenish. I had glimpsed the fellow before at Court and we knew each other by sight and reputation. I was surprised by his intense dislike of me, well hidden, only his eyes betraying him.

'My Lord,' he began abruptly. 'You are here about the Princes?'

'How do you know?'

The doctor raised his eyebrows.

'Obvious. We live in a small community. Rumours abound. Men confide in physicians. Moreover, you are one of the King's right-hand men. I am sure,' he added sarcastically, 'the King has not sent you on a courtesy visit.'

'You saw the Princes, Sir Giles?'

'Yes, the last time was a week before Brackenbury arrived. The younger one, York,' he added, 'was

45

subdued, quiet, pitiful.' The physician paused, weaving his fingers together in agitation. 'Prince Edward,' he continued, 'was suffering from an abscess of the gum. He was melancholic, regarding every day as his last, regularly making his confession.' His words chilled me. I thought of the two princes in that dreadful chamber.

'So he expected to die?'

'Yes,' Argentine replied. 'He often said that he hoped that now his uncle had taken his crown, he would at least leave him his life.' The physician's hostility was now obvious as if he found my presence obnoxious.

'Sir Giles.' I forced him to look at me. 'You do not know me. Yet you regard me as an enemy.'

'This is a sham!' The words were spat out. 'This, this,' Argentine snapped, 'asking me questions about the Princes. What do you care? You are one of the King's henchmen, you already know the truth!'

'I do not, sir, nor does the King!' I snapped back. I nodded, rose and left abruptly, not caring whether he took offence or not. On the one hand I felt angry but on the other quite disgusted and frightened at the task the King had entrusted to me. I sent a servant to fetch Brackenbury to meet me in the Tower gardens. He came soon enough and I told him I was leaving. For one moment I thought he was going to say something but he remained tight-lipped and, spinning on his heel, strode away.

I walked back through the different gateways and down to the quayside. I hailed a skiff which was pulling away. The shrivelled-faced waterman turned and smiled, but his abrupt change of expression and the slight crunch on the gravel behind made me turn, just in time to see the assassin edge towards me, like a spider scurrying out of the darkness. Dressed completely in black, with a hood pulled over his face, he carried both sword and dagger. I drew my own and feinted as the assailant closed with me. One, two parries, our breaths coming in short gasps, our feet scuffing the gravel; I heard the shouts of the boatman and the annoyed cawing of the ravens. My body was soaked in sweat. I am an indifferent swordsman and was frightened on how the attack would end. We closed once more; my assailant thrust and parried with sword and dagger, our blades striking in a sharp clash of steel. Suddenly I heard shouting. I glimpsed Belknap running down the trackway from the Tower gate, behind him members of the garrison. The assassin closed once more but I pushed him off. Belknap was now near. The fellow feinted, dodged by me and took to his heels, running like the wind along the riverbank towards the city.

Belknap was all concerned, talking in sharp bursts of breath; how he had returned to the Tower, learnt I had just left and come after me, calling out the soldiers when he saw the attack. I thanked him profusely, leaving him to dismiss the soldiers while I called the skiff in. We climbed aboard, the wizened, gap-toothed boatman all agog with questions. Belknap told him to mind his own business and soon we were in mid-stream heading back towards Abbots Place near Westminster Palace. Belknap was silent; I, still trembling, relieved at my narrow escape. Someone had sent that assailant after me. But who? Brackenbury? Argentine? One of Buckingham's men? The agent Percivalle? Slaughter, the man I would have to search for? Or had he been sent by one of the many factions who hated King Richard and any of his supporters?

To be truthful, I wondered about Howard himself, even Richard. By the time we reached Westminster Hall, I was calm but quietly furious. I expected to find Norfolk but was informed he had returned to Crosby Place. So, using my authority and the King's warrant, I immediately hired horses and, skirting the city, travelled via Aldgate, up into Bishopsgate and Crosby Place. Once again I thanked Belknap, that most honourable of servants, that most faithful of retainers, with a bag of silver and searched out Howard. My anger only grew for the Duke had left, being busy sitting at the Guildhall with Royal Justices hearing cases. Still hooded and cloaked, though accompanied by my six retainers, I made my way through the city using all my authority and the presence of my retinue to push my way through the noisy, smelly throng. No apprentice dared run out to me offering geegaws, lace ribbons or hot pies. The sight of my livery and the naked steel of my escort soon cleared a path. I strode into the Guildhall, pushing aside bailiffs, officials with their white wands of office, telling them I was on the King's business.

Norfolk was in the main chamber, seated behind a green baize table, his fellow-justices arranged on each side of him. To his left was the scriptorium, where sweating clerks recorded what was being said, whilst soldiers dressed in blue, wearing the white lion rampant of Norfolk, brought both plaintiffs and defendants up to the bar to be heard. I dare not interrupt. Norfolk dismissed me, his mouth hard and angry, his eyes beseeching for no public dispute about the King's secret matter. I calmed down and sat on a bench, watching the Duke's quick and summary justice. Two men to be hanged at the Elms for murder and rape; another to be branded with an 'F' for forgery; two river pirates to be hanged on the riverbank, their bodies to dangle there for seven turns of the tide; a man who wished to leave sanctuary and abjure the realm; and, finally, a fraudulent relic-seller, who claimed he owned the foreskin of some obscure saint. The court dissolved in laughter when the city official plaintively stated that the fellow had sold the same relic over sixty times. Norfolk bellowed out how this indeed was a miracle for how many foreskins did even a saint have! The man was sentenced to a week in the stocks. Norfolk announced the court was adjourned, rose and went off into a small chamber. I followed him there. He took off his red robe, fringed with lambswool, replacing it with a velvet gown, and began to bandage his forehead with a piece of white linen.

'Ten kernels of pepper ground in vinegar,' he muttered. 'Physicians say it is a sure remedy for headaches.' He peered at me slyly and I realised he was frightened.

'You look angry, Lovell!' he snapped. 'Out with it, man. What is the matter?'

I angrily questioned him about his visit to the Tower but Norfolk dismissed it as a matter of courtesy. He had rights there as Constable of England; it was his duty to visit the place.

'And Slaughter?' I asked. 'Black Will, the Princes' only servant and gaoler?'

Norfolk shrugged. 'I sent Slaughter there,' he muttered. 'Because the King ordered it. Someone from my household. Someone who never knew the Princes and could not be suborned. I agreed. He seemed a sensible enough fellow and he was one less mouth to feed in my own household.' Norfolk suddenly pulled out his dagger and, turning, cut a capon pie which was on a platter on a table behind him.

'Here!' he said. 'I have answered your questions. Now eat. It will settle your humours.'

I accepted, mollified by Norfolk's generosity, but he must have read the silent accusation in my eyes. Poor, bluff Norfolk. He dismissed the matter of the Princes as of little import, more worried and concerned about the growing restlessness and conspiracies in London and the surrounding shires. I was about to leave when suddenly I remembered Slaughter and made one last request of him. The Duke looked surprised but agreed, saying he would send the information to Crosby Place as soon as it was available.

After my meeting with Norfolk, I set off for

Westminster. If the Princes were missing or dead, then surely their mother, Elizabeth Woodville, would know something about it? The former Queen, on hearing of Richard's seizure of her elder son at the end of April, had lost her nerve. She broke into great lamentations, bewailing her child's ruin, her friends' mischance and her own misfortunes. She immediately took sanctuary in the abbott's lodging at Westmister, taking with her the nine-year-old Duke of York and her considerable bevy of daughters. Her son by her first marriage, Thomas Grey, Marquis of Dorset, had made a feeble attempt to protect her but quickly lost heart and joined his mother at Westminster. Avaricious as ever, Elizabeth had insisted on taking as many of her possessions as possible, chests, coffers, packs, bundles. Once there, she had squatted like a serving-girl on the rushes, all desolate and despairing. She did not trust her brother-in-law, Richard of Gloucester, loudly cursing him and saying he was dedicated to destroying both her and her blood. Two weeks later, under pressure from the Archbishop of Canterbury, Cardinal Bourchier, and the silent menaces of the Duke of Norfolk, she had given up her younger son, saying with considerable pathetic insight, 'Farewell, my sweet son. Let me kiss you once more, for only God knows when we shall kiss again.'

I should have felt sorry for the stupid woman but I always have, and always will, consider her the real cause of all our problems. She had driven a wedge between Edward and his brothers, Richard and George of Clarence, allowed her brood of relatives the richest pickings in both church and state, and alienated everyone by her arrogance. I had seen her feasting alone, seated on a throne of gold in a chamber bedecked with silks and silver clothes, while her own mother and the King's sister had to kneel whenever they wished to speak to her. Now she was in sanctuary, the Marquis of

Dorset, soon tiring of his mother, escaped from Westminster. The King had the surrounding country-side cordoned off by troops who searched the fields and woodlands with dogs but without success. The Marquis reached France and, so the King had confided in me, the ex-queen kept up constant communication with him.

In an attempt to forestall this as well as to prevent any future escapes, the King had the abbey cordoned off, entrusting the command to one of his own body squires, John Nesfield. I met the latter as soon as I arrived at the abbey, a northerner, a born soldier and swordsman. Stocky, sharp-tongued, his corn-coloured hair cropped close about his head, he, and over a hundred archers dressed in chain-mail and steel caps, had surrounded the abbey entrances, lighting the night with the flames of their camp-fires. Once he knew the reason for my visit, he allowed me entrance into the cloisters. I sent a message with one of the monks that I wished words with the Lady Elizabeth. She delayed her coming so long that I thought she was refusing to see me, but eventually she came down. Dressed completely in black, her head-dress a mist of dark veils, she looked a shadow of her former self. Her face, once olive and heart-shaped, was now white, podgy and soaked with tears; those beautiful eyes which had enraptured and ensnared Edward of York were red-rimmed with constant crying. She was accompanied by her eldest daughter, also called Elizabeth, who was similarly dressed; a glimpse of her face and large grey eyes reminded me of her mother's former beauty.

The ex-queen and I knew each other of old. I disliked her, and she hated me, not because I had given her any offence, she simply detested anyone who consorted with Richard of Gloucester. Her whole body and stance betrayed this rancour. She stopped a few paces from me, her black-gloved hand constantly dabbing at her eyes with a white lace handkerchief. She was supported by her daughter and seemed to be on the verge of collapsing in a faint.

'You wished to see me, Lovell?' I walked closer but she held her hand up. 'No further.' I studied her closely, this most arrogant of women who had fallen like a star from heaven.

'Madame,' I said softly. 'I bring you greetings from His Grace the King.' The Woodville woman smirked and I knew there was something wrong. Of course she was distressed, but there was pretence here, hypocrisy. She must have heard the rumours and I expected her to be hysterical. Did she, I wondered, know something secret from anyone else? I looked at her proud face, a flickering shadow in the light of the cloister torches.

'Madame?' I asked. 'You have nothing to say?'

'Sir,' she replied. 'I know well there are rumours. My sons, they have gone. Maybe …' Her voice faltered.

'Who told you that, Madame?'

'Rumours are like birds!' she snapped. 'They fly where they wish. From servants, lay brothers, the chatter of the abbey.'

'Madame, do you know anything about your sons?' I asked. She stepped forward, brushing aside her daughter's supporting arm, no need now for any support. Her eyes glittered, her carmine-painted lips curled back like some snarling cur.

'If I did know something!' she hissed, 'I would prefer my sons to be in hell than to tell your master!' Her voice rose. 'He has despoiled my state, stripped me of my possessions, proclaimed my sons bastards and my marriage bigamous! For God's sake, get out of my sight!' She turned, her skirts billowing with the fury of her movements, and stalked away. Her daughter, throwing one contemptuous look at me, followed her back into the abbey.

Six

I returned to Crosby Place and went to my chamber, preparing to itemise what I had learnt, but I was too tired, fearful and anxious. I wrote a short note to my wife, my beloved Anne, and packed a small gift I had bought for her from a goldsmith in Cheapside. I opened a casement window to let in the night air and stood breathing the fragance of the flower gardens whilst wondering what to do next. Eventually, I doused the candle and, still fully dressed, fell asleep on the bed. When I awoke it was dark. The room was cold and I was alarmed because the candle had been moved, lit and placed on a trunk at the foot of the huge four-poster bed. Still half-asleep I was about to douse it when I heard the click of a crossbow. I peered into the circle of light and saw a shadow move.

'Who is there?' I called out.

'Be still, my Lord.' The voice was soft but menacing. I sat up, my back to the bolsters, my hand searching under the coverlet for the fine, razor-sharp knife I always kept with me at night.

'Your dagger is here!' I saw the glint of steel and heard the dagger as it fell with a soft thud to the carpet. 'No need to be afraid, my Lord. I simply bring messages.'

'From whom?'

'Oh, from different people who wish you no ill but regret your present allegiance.'

'Why should they do that?' I asked, staring into the darkness, trying to catch a glimpse of my midnight visitor.

'Because,' this time I caught the sing-song tongue of the speaker, more suited to a troubador or story-teller than a possible assassin. 'Because it will lead to perdition. We hunt the boar, my Lord, and though it may swerve, turn, fight or hide in the deepest thickets, we will root it out.'

'The King is crowned,' I replied. 'He is much loved.'

'The King is a usurper,' came the tart reply. 'Who cares for old Dickon with his smooth smiles and false gestures? He is an assassin and has been from the start.'

'You mean the Princes?' I regretted the words as soon as they were out of my mouth.

'Oh, the Princes, they are gone.' The fellow sniggered. 'I mean much worse than that. His own brother, my Lord, the late, dead King Edward, taken ill suddenly whilst boating on the Thames.'

'Richard of Gloucester was in the north at the time.'

'Oh yes,' the fellow replied. 'But his agents were here. Why not ask them? On the same night King Edward died, even before dawn, one of Richard's agents, Mistlebrook, hastened to the house of a man called Potyer. He dwells in Red Cross Street near Cripplegate. Mistlebrook told Potyer that the King was dead. Do you know what Potyer's reply was, Lovell?' The mysterious visitor did not wait for my answer. 'Potyer said "By my troth, man, then my master, the Duke of Gloucester, will be King." Now, my Lord Lovell, do you not think it is strange? Here is an ordinary citizen of London. He knows when the King died and immediately hastens to one of Richard's agents to give him the news.'

I stared into the blackness; my visitor's words vexed me, for I knew Richard Potyer. He was an attorney in the Duchy of Lancaster's chancery, and before that, when Richard was Duke of Gloucester, Potyer had been the Princes' attorney in the court of chancery.

'Oh, there's more,' my visitor whispered. 'No doubt, my Lord, you will be returning north, back to the White Boar's den. The city of York where the usurper vaunts he is loved so much. Make enquiries, Lovell, especially at the church of St. Peter's. You will find a Mass was offered up there for the repose of King Edward's soul two days before he actually died. Make other enquiries. You will find Duke Richard was preparing arms and men long before his brother died, using the war with Scotland as a pretext for his secret preparations.'

'Why do you tell me this,' I asked, 'when only a few hours ago you sent an assassin to kill me?'

'I sent no assassin,' came the cool reply. 'You see, my Lord, you do not know your friends from your enemies. I merely come to tell you this, to make you think. To consider wisely whether Richard of Gloucester is as sure on this throne as he thinks he is.'

'You are Percivalle, are you not?'

'Yes, I am Percivalle, my Lord, and perhaps we shall meet again.' The candle was suddenly extinguished. I heard the room door open and close. I jumped from my bed but, fumbling around in the dark, by the time I opened the chamber door and looked along the darkened passageway, there was nothing but the usual creak of timber and the howl of a dog in the far distance of the night. I went back, lit the candles and, taking pen and a scrap of vellum, began to itemise what I had learnt.

Item – Richard of Gloucester had seized the throne. He proclaimed his own brother's marriage as bigamous and therefore his nephews, the young princes, were bastards with no claims to the throne.

Item – Richard had brutally executed all those who dared oppose him: Lord Hastings and leading members of the young prince's council; and the Earl Rivers, Lord Richard Grey, Sir Thomas Vaughan and Sir Richard

Hawkes, who were beheaded at Pontefract, their naked bodies thrown into a common grave.

Item – The two young princes had been placed in the Tower, given a certain amount of freedom but eventually shut up in the keep.

Item – The Princes had been withdrawn from public view, their servants had been dismissed. They were confined to a chamber in the turret in the White Tower, being served by only one man, William Slaughter, a retainer of the Duke of Norfolk.

Item – Sir Robert Brackenbury seems to be innocent of any violence against the bastard princes, yet he is evidently ill at ease and appears to be concealing something.

Item – The Tower was visited by three members of Richard's council: Norfolk, Buckingham and Sir James Tyrrell, the King's Master of Horse, his principal henchman, who came to the Tower some days before Brackenbury noticed the princes had vanished.

Item – There are rumours about the Princes being dead but the agent Percivalle evaded this issue whilst the Woodville woman, their mother, seemed not too distressed. Surely, if the Princes were dead and such information had been communicated to her, she would have become hysterical?

Item – Finally, is this all a travesty? Has my master the King had the Princes executed? Is he, as Percivalle maintains, an assassin, and has been one from the start? Was he responsible for the murder of his own kin, laying down a well devised stratagem to remove his brother and then his nephews from the throne?

I sat back on the bed, looking up at the red-gold canopy above me. I thought of Richard, not as a King but as my fellow-squire years ago at Middleham Castle. Perhaps that was my weakness, I constantly saw the boy and not the man. I thought of Richard as I had last seen him at Minster Lovell, his face pale and pinched, gnawing his lower lip, the eyes hooded, the small wiry body tense with nervous energy. Did Richard also put his trust in the bonds of boyhood? Did he believe I could be duped, using me as a pawn to show his household and Court that he was no murderer, no spiller of innocent blood? Events earlier in the year crossed my mind. They seemed an age away, in that happy time when I was a henchman in the Duke of Gloucester's household and happy to be so. Oh, we all knew Edward was dying. His great frame sodden by drink, his belly sagging like a pregnant woman's, but his brain had still been razor-sharp, the cornflower blue eyes confident and assertive. But then he died suddenly. Had it been poison? Was Richard responsible? The conversation between Potyer and Mistlebrook could have been treasonable but, there again, Richard had no choice but to assert himself. He openly told us so in those secret council meetings held in Middleham Castle after the news of his brother's death. Time and again he had shown us what would happen; how the Woodvilles would dominate London, control the Tower, the Courts, the Exchequer, the Armouries and the Treasure Houses. How the Queen's other son, the Marquis of Dorset, had the fleet in his grasp. Her able and efficient brother, the Earl Rivers, had the young Edward in Wales and would pour honeyed poison into the young prince's ear about his other uncle far away in the north.

I, like Ratcliffe, Catesby and Tyrrell, had agreed Richard should move; we were all swept up in the excitement: Richard's secret alliance with Buckingham and Hastings, the seizure of the young prince at Stony Stratford, the imprisonment of Rivers and the turbulent march on London. The sudden collapse of the Woodville party seemed to indicate that God was with us and after that, like knights charging in battle, we were carried forward by the force and speed of our own

movements. Richard could never give up the Protectorship and then, as an answer to a prayer, Bishop
Stillington of Bath and Wells had declared King
Edward IV's and Elizabeth Woodville's marriage to be
bigamous. The Princes were bastard issue and, as in the
twinkling of an eye, Richard seized the crown.

I had been party to this. Oh, yes, as I now stare death
in its skull-like face, I admit I had reservations, secret
doubts, but I buried these. Yet, sitting in that upper
chamber in Crosby Hall, I had to face fresh doubts. Was
Richard an assassin? Was he a consummate actor and
liar? The safest answer would have been that he was,
and in two days I could have been at one of the Cinque
ports and across the narrow seas to Brittany. Yet I had
other doubts. Why should Richard murder two young
princes? Their deaths would only alienate the people.
Yet, even if he had issued the order, would a man like
Brackenbury, even though he was new in his office as
Constable of the Tower, agree to such a task?

I looked at the other possibility. Did the Princes
escape? Not by themselves, two young boys could never
effect that. There were three possibilities. First Black
Will, the varlet Slaughter, might have abducted them.
Tyrrell might have done likewise, but why? A
dangerous, volatile man. Sir James was loyal to King
Richard. The only other possibility could be
Buckingham. This over-ambitious Duke was now
plotting against the King. Had he used his visit to the
Tower to abduct the prisoners? I cleared my mind of all
doubts and fastened on this. If Buckingham had taken
the Princes, this would account for the Woodville
woman's lack of real concern; then he surely would have
sent them abroad? Not to Brittany. He would not hand
such powerful pawns over to the Tudor. The safest
place would be the court of the grasping, shrewd, spider
king, Louis XI of France.

The next morning I kept to my chamber, constantly

reviewing my conclusions. I dismissed Percivalle's visit for the time being as mischievous. I was certain that similar approaches must have been made to other members of Richard's entourage (in this I was proved right). The most interesting aspect of the spy's meeting with me was his hint that the Princes might still be alive, which confirmed my belief that they might well be in France. I called Belknap to my chamber. He came wary-eyed and watchful. I made no reference to recent happenings but told him how I wished him to travel immediately to France. He was to bear messages of good will from the Chamberlain of King Richard's household to Louis XI and his Court.

Richard had already sent his herald, Blanc Sanglier, to Plessis-les-Tours, and another envoy, Doctor Norton. Belknap's mission, however, was to be informal; he was to collect information, particularly any knowledge on the part of the French about the young princes. He was to be discreet, expeditious and secretive. Surprisingly, Belknap seemed happy with such a mission. I told him that the necessary letters, warrants and credentials would be ready. He was to leave as quickly as possible and report to me by letter, if his journey home be hampered.

After Belknap had left, I met once again with the Duke of Norfolk. We discussed general matters, particularly the conspiracies in London and the surrounding shires. Howard was insistent he move back into East Anglia where he could more easily call up levies. We considered the possibility of arresting Buckingham but I agreed with the Duke that such a venture would be highly dangerous and quite impossible to execute. Instead, we decided letters should be sent north to the King, advising him of Buckingham's treachery and the growing discontent in the south.

I hung around London for days kicking my heels whilst waiting for the information I had requested from

Norfolk. At last it came. Roll after roll of coroners'
reports, listing those people found dead in the city
between the 27th July and the beginning of August. I
had chosen those dates deliberately; the man I was
seeking had either fled from London or, on the basis
that he knew too much about the secret plans of the
great ones of the kingdom, would have been brutally
murdered. The lists made sombre reading: men and
women killed by sickness, accidents or some fierce
affray – but most were named, well-known in their
wards, whilst those who were classed as strangers were
too old to fit the description of the man I was looking
for. Eventually, I noticed one. A young man, a stranger,
whose throat had been cut, the corpse dumped in a
small alleyway off Cheapside.

I promptly sought an interview with the Duke of
Norfolk, now finishing his preparations to leave the
capital. He greeted my arrival with obvious annoyance.
He was tired of answering questions about a matter he
did not give a fig for whilst, as he said, all around us
were seething hotbeds of conspiracy.

'My Lord,' I explained, 'I realise this matter does not
concern you but it does me and, I must remind you, also
the King. Is there anyone in your household, one of
your retinue besides yourself, who could recognise
Slaughter?'

'Why?' The Duke ceased whatever he was doing and
came close. 'Why, Lovell? What is the matter?'

'I have examined the coroners' rolls and believe I
have found the corpse of a man who matches
Slaughter's description. He was found on the night of
August 2nd near Cheapside and has been interred in a
pauper's grave in St. Botolph's churchyard outside
Newgate. I intend to exhume that body, my Lord, and I
want someone to view the corpse.'

Norfolk shrugged, and calling his servant, asked him
to send for John Howstead, the sub-controller of the

household. Howstead was a young, dour, bitter-faced fellow who greeted my request with dark looks and bitter muttering. However, when the Duke rapped out an order, the fellow grudgingly agreed to accompany me.

Seven

I remember it was a hot day. The streets were packed and the stench was so offensive I kept a nosegay to my face, as much to ward the smells off as provide a disguise. I had also arranged for two workmen from Crosby Hall to accompany three of my retainers, placed a good few paces behind me as protection against any attack. It was a long, hot walk, down Cheapside through the offal and rubbish of the Shambles, past Newgate prison to St. Botolph's Church. A dark area of the city. Many of the prostitutes who plied their trade in the locality stood in darkened doorways, hair dyed, faces heavily painted, calling out lewd invitations to us as we passed. Howstead, his face plum-coloured with embarrassment, kept up muttered complaints but eventually shut up when I stopped and glared menacingly at him.

The priest of St. Botolph's answered my pounding at his door. At first he was going to refuse, his poxed, sallow features suffused with righteous indignation. He scratched his shoulder-length, greasy hair and considered my request. Finally, I produced both my dagger and the general warrant from the King. The fellow quickly agreed and, after consulting a book he brought back to the doorway, led me and my companions across the overgrown churchyard to a desolate, shady spot beneath a huge overhanging elm tree.

'The fellow was buried here,' he mumbled. 'I forget exactly where.' He smiled, showing a row of blackened teeth. 'I remember the grave was shallow for the ground was hard to break up. It will be even harder now.' I gestured to the workmen to begin digging. The priest was right, the ground was iron-hard, and the labourers quietly cursed each other, the task, and, with angry glances at me, high and mighty lords. Time and again they uncovered some pathetic sight, the coffin of a small baby or the yellowing skeleton of some derelict. Howstead, unable to bear these sights, walked away. After a while so did I, standing in the cool porch of the church until the shouts and cries of the priest brought me back.

'They have found your corpse, my Lord,' the fellow observed sardonically. 'Come! Have a look!' I moved over, noticing the face of one of the workmen was almost a whitish-green. They had disinterred a shapeless canvas bundle. I took my dagger and, holding the nosegay over my nose and mouth, cut the cheap canvas covering. The corpse lay as it had been buried, naked except for a loincloth, any clothes or jewellery having been stripped by either the priest or those who had buried the body. The stench, even after a few days, was rank and offensive and I had to stop myself gagging. The eyes were shut but the mouth yawned open, the skin dirty, puffy-white and damp; from ear to ear ran a long purple gash. I called Howstead over. He took one look, turned away to vomit, nodding his head in recognition.

'That's Slaughter!' he gasped. 'God damn you but that is Slaughter!' I patted him gently on the shoulder, tossing coins to both the priest and the labourers.

'Take care of the corpse,' I said. 'Howstead, come with me.'

Outside the churchyard I questioned Howstead carefully. Satisfied with the information, I dismissed him and ordered my three retainers who were waiting there, to follow me at a safe distance. I was glad to be free of that evil churchyard and Howstead's mournful company, pleased to be in the sun even though I had to make my way through narrow streets, dirty, greasy and darkened by the houses packed next to each other. The upper tiers were gilted and gabled, jutting out to block the sunlight, built according to chance and hazard rather than any set plan.

I thought of Anne, fresh-faced, vivacious, the cool chambers of Minster Lovell and the lush greenness of its meadowlands. I was tired of London, quietly cursing the King's task. At last we were back into Cheapside, amongst the stalls, booths, the shop fronts lowered, hanging by chains, the constant din of the tradesmen behind me.

'Fresh fish!' 'Sweet plums!' 'Apples fresh off the branch!' 'Portions of hot meat!' 'Wines from Alsace!' Apprentices plucked at my arm, trying to inveigle my custom, but I kept my head down and they let me go with strange oaths and cries of 'Go, by cock!'

Sitting here alone, I realise the contrariness of human nature. Then, I wished to be in Minster Lovell, now I desire to be back in Cheapside with the sun blazing above me and the press of people about me so great I found it difficult to walk. I am sorry – I break my pledge not to look back with the great wisdom of hindsight. At that time I was afraid of being attacked so I kept my face down, taking care to avoid the lords, the young gallants in their silk doublets with fiercely padded shoulders and high waists, their sleeves puffed out in concoctions of velvet, damask and satin. Such men were dangerous; one of them might have recognised me and not every courtier in London, as Norfolk and I knew, was loyal to King Richard. At last I turned off Cheapside, down a number of side-streets, past houses fair and foul. I skirted the Poultry, where the stench of offal from the slaughter-houses made me feel nauseous as I remembered the corpse I had just viewed.

I entered Farringdon Ward, crossing the great stinking cattle-market of Smithfield and into the cool darkness of the tavern, the one Howstead had directed me to, 'The Sun in Splendour'. The landlord came bustling up, one calloused hand combing back his dank, rat-tailed hair. I looked at his watery eyes and yellow buckteeth and wished to God the business was over and I was gone. I ordered a pot of ale and asked to see his daughter. The man grinned and was about to nudge me as if I was some fellow-conspirator but I glared at him and moved away to sit in a corner. His daughter, Isabella, was a pleasing contrast, tidily dressed, her dark hair pinned up under her veil. She was sweet-faced, eager to please until I mentioned Slaughter's name. She was about to move away but I ordered her to sit down.

'I mean you no harm, mistress,' I said. 'But you were sweet on Master Slaughter, or Black Will as he was known?' The girl nodded, her eyes brimming with tears.

'Why do you say "was", Sir?' she asked. 'Has anything happened to him?'

'No. No,' I lied. 'You were the only person he talked to?' She nodded. 'Did he ever tell you about his tasks?' She shook her head. 'When did you see him last?' I asked gently. The girl looked down at her hands.

'Ten, twelve days ago,' she whispered. 'Yes, I remember, the 1st of August. It was the beginning of the month. In the evening. He came here, furtive and restless. He left and I have not seen him since.' I looked into her childlike grey eyes and believed that of all the people I had questioned in London, she was telling the truth. I dug into my purse and, taking out a gold coin, pressed it into the palm of her hand. She thanked me with her eyes.

'Sir,' she said quietly. 'Do you know where Slaughter is? Will he return?'

'No,' I lied, not bothering to turn. 'No, I do not know where he is, but I do not think he will ever return.'

I returned to Crosby Hall convinced that Slaughter's death had something to do with the Princes' disappearance. I also felt my work in London was finished. Any further stay would only endanger myself and raise more questions. Norfolk left London on the 11th, Belknap had already gone, so I ordered my retainers to pack and on the 14th left London, riding hard and fast along the old Roman road, on to the country lanes past Banbury to Minster Lovell. I was pleased to be free of the city. The summer had been long and golden, the corn was ready for harvest and the birdsong on the clear air warmed my heart. After two days of travel I entered the green lush fields of my manor. I glimpsed the red-tiled roof and yellow bricked walls of the Minster and heard the sweet gurgling sound of the Windrush as it flowed between green banks down to turn the wheel of an old cornmill.

Anne was waiting for me as I had sent a retainer ahead. She came running into the yard, her long hair streaming in the soft breeze, throwing her arms round my neck before I had scarcely dismounted. Poor Anne! Sweet Anne! If we had only known the terrors which lay ahead of us. The church is right to condemn and castigate those who attempt to divine the future.

I am sure that if we knew we would lose the will to live. Nonetheless, these days of dalliance at Minster Lovell were some of the sweetest in my life. Anne had used my new-found wealth to decorate and beautify the hall: new beeswax candles in the candlebeams, diamond-shaped glass in the windows of our chamber, a huge new bed standing on a dais with four gilt posts and draped by a cloth of velvet and gold, embroidered with the silver dogs of my escutcheon. We used the bed soon enough, laughing and teasing one another. Anne pointed out the new drapes she had bought, the cloth of red-gold arras depicting the scene from the Bible, 'Susannah and the Judges', as well as the new chairs

covered with red leather bearing the silver-white dog of
the Lovells. I teased Anne for being a spendthrift but
she only laughed all the more, claiming she had bought
most of the materials before I left Minster Lovell. She
had kept them hidden, wanting to surprise me.

We spent days walking in the huge garden which lies
at the back of the manor, sitting on the bank of the
Windrush, the fragrance of white lilies, marjoram and
wine-dark roses as sweet as any perfume about us.
Other times I helped her in the herb garden. She taught
me the difference between lavender, hyssop, penny-
royal, camomile and other sweet-smelling flowers and
herbs. At night, long banquets with only the two of us as
guests, as we ate young porpoise, salted hart, lampreys,
quails, venison pastries, baked quinces and goblet after
goblet of different wines. She would tease me all the
time, especially with riddles. Now, seated near the great
hall where she and I loved and kissed, I can almost hear
her voice, bubbling with laughter, calling out her
favourite riddle:

A pot I have

It is rounded like a pear.

Moist in the middle,

Surrounded with hair.

And often it happens

That water flows there.

She would not tell me the answer, but now, the tears
wet on my cheeks, I smile for I knew she referred to the
eye.

I had not told Anne about the King's task. I did not

wish to trouble her with the sludge and filth of the Court, but at times her gaiety was brittle. I would catch her looking at me, carefully, guardedly. I would smile and she would chatter on about her father, Lord Fitzhugh, or the business and affairs of her sisters. One night as we lay beneath the red-gold canopy of the bed, she turned, stroking my face, and asked:

'Francis, I know there is something wrong.' She propped herself up on her elbow. 'It is the King,' she said, looking down at me. 'I have heard the rumours and gossip, Francis,' she continued. 'Men plot and conspire constantly against him. I do not worry about Richard, but should he fall he will take you with him.'

'Yet the King has raised me up,' I replied. 'Our family emblem is a dog, but one which hunts, not runs at the slightest sign of danger,' and, gathering her into my arms, I refused to talk any further.

The following day I prepared to leave, discussing with Anne the different accounts of the manor and our other holdings in Yorkshire and Nottingham. I refused to fix a date for my return. I remembered our conversation the previous evening and gave her strict instructions that if things went untoward, she was to flee Minster Lovell and seek sanctuary with her father. Once I knew she had left the hall on some errand or other, I went to my secret chamber built behind the great fireplace. My father had devised this place when rebuilding the hall, a small room behind the great hearth where I kept a number of valuables, private papers and documents. There, in a coffer, I placed the memoranda I had drawn up in London about the King's secret task.

I left Minster Lovell late that same afternoon and, accompanied by my retainers, travelled to the King at Pontefract where he was preparing for his great entrance into the city of York. His Grace's love of York was well-known and he looked forward to his visits as any child does to a mummer's play at Christmas. He was too busy and excited to converse with me. His wife, Anne (the young Neville heiress), and his only son, Edward, had also joined him but when I saw these I secretly despaired. The Queen was thin, emaciated, her once rounded face was white, almost sallow and she was constantly racked by convulsive fits of coughing. The young prince was no better; a pale shadow of his father, he was weak, listless, and had to be conveyed everywhere in a specially constructed horse-litter. There were others of the Court present: William Catesby, Sir Richard Ratcliffe and Sir James Tyrrell. The latter looked at me strangely and I suspected the smiles on their fox-like faces hid a deep curiosity about my whereabouts. The only person beside the King who seemed genuinely joyful was Richard's ubiquitous and loyal secretary, John Kendall; he informed me how the burgesses of York had been preparing for a month to welcome Richard, how the mayor and aldermen had already sent the King gifts of wine, cygnets, herons and rabbits.

On Saturday, August 30th, King Richard and Prince Edward, with a huge retinue, myself included, entered York. We were preceded by two sheriffs of the city who rode at the head of a long procession, each bearing their silver wands of office. At Breckles Mills, just outside the city walls, the mayor, aldermen and councillors, dressed in a wild profusion of red and scarlets, greeted the royal family. They took us into the city through Micklegate to be cheered by a mass of citizens clad in blue and gold velvet, the favourite colours of the city. As we went under the gate I saw Richard look up; for a moment his face went grim as he remembered his own father, Duke Richard, and elder brother, Edmund, who had been caught and trapped by a Lancastrian army just outside Wakefield. Both father and son had been killed, their heads hacked off, crowned with paper hats and placed above Micklegate Bar. Richard had never forgotten their deaths, determined not to forfeit the hard-earned rewards of the House of York.

The procession wound its way to the Guildhall, the King and his retinue being taken up by a series of banquets and receptions, amid a never-ending swirl of silk, trumpetings, speeches and exchanges of gifts. On Sunday September 7th, we attended his favourite drama, the Creed play, performed by the Corpus Christi Guild. The following day Richard's son was installed as Prince of Wales in a gorgeous multi-coloured ceremony in York Cathedral. I watched the pageant, thinking Richard had forgotten the task he had entrusted to me, but that was Richard, publicly playing the role of the popular King whilst all the time scurriers, messengers and spies were sent south to bring back information about the conspiracies brewing there. Nor had he forgotten the secret matter. On that same Sunday evening he convoked a meeting of his secret council in a small chamber in the Archbishop's house in York.

I remember it was dark. A thunderstorm had swept in from the sea and fat, heavy drops of rain pelted the stain-glass windows of the room. Beeswax candles dipped, winked and glittered on silver and gold ornaments, catching and fanning the glow of a precious diamond necklace, ruby ring or some other valuable stone. Richard sat at the head of a long trestle-table, on his left his principal councillors. There was Sir Richard Ratcliffe, a fierce fighter from Westmoreland, knighted for his bloody service at Tewkesbury. A seafarer, Ratcliffe had terrorised the Scots off Galloway; a man of shrewd wit, short and rude of speech and temper. He was bold in mischief and as far from pity as from fear of God. Next to him, William Catesby, Richard's Chancellor of the Exchequer, a lawyer from Northampton, a man who served Lord William Hastings but, when

Hastings fell, Catesby switched his allegiance. A shrewd, hard-visaged man but a popinjay. He kept peacocks on his estate and loved to wear costly raiment, white or green satin doublets, scarlet hose, black leather Spanish riding-boots to which he always fastened spurs which jingled and clinked whenever he moved. Then Sir James Tyrrell, the only southerner, Master of Horse and the King's henchman, red-haired, foxy-faced, a sharp contrast to the last person, Sir Edward Brampton, a Portuguese Jew and former pirate. He had been converted to the true faith, no less a person than King Edward IV standing as godfather. He was dark, swarthy, his oiled hair hanging in ringlets about his face. He always insisted on wearing crimson and scarlet and liked to fasten little bells to his clothes so that he walked constantly in a shimmer of silvery noise. I looked at each one of those present. God forgive my evil suspicions but, at the time, I thought they might all be murderers.

Eight

Richard began the meeting, giving a sharp, decisive description of the conspiracy in the south, expressing anxiety about how Buckingham not only refused to answer his letters but dismissed Richard's messengers with total disdain. Haltingly, he began to talk about the Princes, sometimes making mistakes, calling them his true nephews, and then, as if remembering himself, his brother's illegitimate issue. At length, as if tired of the subject, he lapsed into silence and waved a beringed hand at me.

'Francis,' he said, 'perhaps you can give the clearest description of what is happening.'

I told them what I knew. By the end of June, both Princes had been removed to the Tower. The King had visited the fortress on July 4th. On 17 July, Brackenbury had been appointed as Constable and immediately paid his respects to the Princes. The boys had been well, though the elder was morose and withdrawn, suffering from an infection of the jaw. On the 25th, Buckingham had visited them and on the 26th, Brackenbury had seen the Princes again. On the following day Sir James Tyrrell had visited the Tower to collect stores for the King. On the 29th, Brackenbury had discovered them gone and immediately despatched a letter to the King as well as visiting Bishop Russell, the Chancellor.

As I talked, Richard sat slumped in his high-backed

chair, toying with his sparkling ring, refusing to meet my eye. I looked down at the other councillors, their hard, closed faces, and I wondered once again if any of them had been involved in the Princes' disappearance. They were all ruthless men, totally dedicated to Richard; like John Howard, Duke of Norfolk, they viewed the Princes as obstacles to their rise in power and a threat to their own status. I looked sideways at Richard. Was he suffering pangs of guilt? Guilt about murder? Or just guilt for deserting the sons of his own brother? He stirred, chewing his lip.

'My Lords,' he began. 'This matter is no secret, but your advice is needed. What is said here cannot be discussed elsewhere. Whatever you feel or think should now be openly declared.' His words were greeted by silence.

'Sir James Tyrrell,' I asked. 'It is true you visited the Tower?' The fellow nodded. 'And you did not see the Princes?'

'No, I did not.'

'Why?'

Tyrrell shrugged. 'I saw them as of little import.'

'And Brackenbury?' I asked. 'He was well?' Tyrrell stretched out his hand as though examining his fingernails.

'Sir Robert Brackenbury was his usual self. I saw and heard nothing amiss.'

'It's quite simple,' Catesby broke in. 'Surely? The Princes are gone. They have either escaped or been murdered.' He turned towards the King. 'Brackenbury would not commit such an act and certainly not without His Grace's permission. That is so?' Richard nodded. 'Buckingham could not have murdered them,' Catesby continued. 'For they were seen alive after our noble Duke left. The culprit must either be someone we do not know or William Slaughter.'

'But why?' I interrupted. 'Why should Slaughter kill

the Princes? What had he to gain?' Catesby smiled thinly.

'If it was Slaughter,' he murmured, 'then a number of people could have bribed him and, once the act was done, his throat cut.' The room grew quiet. I felt a prickle of sweat on my back. Catesby's conclusions were the same as mine. The last person to have seen the Princes alive was Slaughter. He might well have carried out the dreadful deed but who was behind him? I recollected my conversation with the tavern wench. She had last seen Slaughter on the evening of August 1st. Was that when he had murdered the two boys? Possibly. But the real problem was who had paid him?

Richard's secretary, Kendall, now white-faced, listed the possibilities.

'Your Grace,' he began. 'Slaughter may have been paid by Brackenbury, the Duke of Norfolk, the Duke of Buckingham, or,' he paused, 'anyone in this room.' He held his hands up. 'I mean no disrespect but the crime will be laid at our door.'

'Francis,' the King asked sharply. 'What do you think?'

'Your Grace,' I replied. 'Kendall is correct. I believe the Princes were killed or disappeared around the beginning of August, the same time the rumours began in London and the surrounding shires that the Princes might be murdered. They began,' I added slowly, 'after Buckingham had visited the Princes. Buckingham could have bribed Slaughter to either abduct the Princes or kill them. The fellow did so but was double-crossed, his only reward being a torn throat and a pauper's grave.'

'True! True!' Brampton spoke for the first time, his voice clipped in an attempt to disguise his accent. 'Many men had motives to kill the Princes. Let us be honest. We sit on the council because the Princes were set aside.' He looked quickly at Richard. 'I mean no offence, your Grace. I only say to your face what others relate behind

your back. Buckingham would like them dead.
Remember, as a boy he was a ward of the Woodville
woman, who forced him to marry one of her daughters.
Like us, he hates the entire brood. My Lord of Norfolk
also profits. The Mowbray inheritance was held by the
younger prince; if he was dead I do not think Jack of
Norfolk would weep bitter tears.' He held up one
bejewelled hand. 'We must also remember that my
Lords of Buckingham and Norfolk remained in
London, whereas we joined his Grace's progress
through the country.'

'There is one fly in the ointment,' Catesby interrupted
softly. 'Brackenbury! If anyone had killed the Princes,
Brackenbury would find their corpses. He would tell
the King, as well as inform us of the possible murderer.
I do not believe,' he concluded firmly, 'the Princes are
dead, but that they may have escaped.'

Tempers became heated as different possibilities and
theories were exchanged across the table. I just sat
watching Richard carefully. He still refused to meet my
eye, lost in his own thoughts, impervious to the
discussion. Catesby was right, the key to the solution was
Brackenbury. Was he the murderer? Either on his own
or on secret orders from the King? I quietly promised
myself that Sir Robert and I would certainly discuss the
matter again. Catesby, ever the diplomat, led the
discussion on to the conspiracy in the south and the
possible plans of Buckingham. Adept and skilful, he
drew the King into discussion and Richard vented his
anger and hatred at Buckingham and his coven.

'That man,' Richard shouted, 'has betrayed us all! He
is behind the whispering campaign, spreading malicious
rumours, stories and whatever filth he can dig up. I
believe my Lord Lovell,' he turned and glared at me,
'has other news.' I had told Richard about Percivalle's
meeting with me. The King had dismissed it as a matter
of little consequence yet he had apparently brooded on

the matter, gnawing away at it, imagining threats which did not exist. I had no choice but to describe the scene to the rest of Richard's councillors, the King nodding vigorously as I spoke.

'Percivalle's visit,' the King said menacingly, 'is important. Firstly, because he sows seeds of doubt about my true intentions. Percivalle brought news to me that my brother was dead; he may well have been responsible for rumours that King Edward had died before he actually did. Secondly, Percivalle wished to suborn the allegiance of this,' Richard stretched out a hand and put it lightly on my shoulder, 'my lifelong friend. So, my Lords, if Percivalle has approached Lovell, who else has he visited in the dead of night?' A sharp intake of breath greeted Richard's question. I glanced around. Each of the councillors looked away, shuffling nervously on their chairs. Catesby was the first to reassert himself.

'Your Grace,' he exclaimed. 'I speak for myself and for everyone in this room when I say that our allegiance is to you, and I am prepared to prove my loyalty,' he embraced us in one sweeping gesture, 'as we all do on our bodies.' Amidst such exclamations of loyalty, even anger, at the King's question, the council meeting broke up.

I stayed with the Court at York. The King had private words with me, saying that I was to continue in his secret matter but it would be best if we waited until Buckingham made his move; only then would we gain a clearer picture of what had happened. Meantime the King gave strict orders that all other royal children, including his own bastards, the son of his elder sister and Clarence's simple-minded son, should be moved out of harm's way to Sheriff Hutton in Yorkshire. I do not know why Richard did this. Did he fear some attempt on their lives in a further attempt to blacken his name? At the time I was reassured, but wondered why

Richard had not taken stricter measures over his two nephews.

After his wife and young son left him for Middleham, I approached Richard again in the sacristy of York Cathedral, a place I considered free of any eavesdroppers or spies. The King had paid a private visit to the church and I, as Chamberlain, accompanied him. Seizing the opportunity of being alone, I told him about Brackenbury's nervousness and urged him to do something to counter the rumours about the Princes' death. Despite his secretiveness, I sensed the King's fury and anger.

'I am caught either way, Francis,' he answered hoarsely. 'If I say the Princes have escaped, it gladdens those who constantly plot against me. If I say they are dead, killed by the Duke of Buckingham, who would believe me? They will assert that I am the assassin, eager to pass the blame onto someone else. The same is true of Norfolk. I will still be blamed and lose the support not only of a friend but of my most powerful ally. We are in a dark tunnel, Francis. Ahead of us may be enemies and snares. We must walk silently, create no stir.' He paused and grasped me firmly by the arm. 'But for my sake, Francis, my own peace of soul, I must know what happened to those boys. Where are they? Are they to appear in a year, two years' time, backed by France, Brittany, Burgundy or the Empire to challenge my rule and that of my son? You are to keep with this task, Francis, and not give it up until we have found the truth. I have your word?'

'You have my word, your Grace.'

Two days later I received the following letter from Belknap in France; it dashed other hopes:

'Thomas Belknap, steward, to Francis, Viscount Lovell, health and greetings. Know you how my journey to France was both swift and safe and that I have come to the French King's Court at Plessis-les-Tours.

However, Monsieur the King of France is, so common report has it, now dying and refuses to meet anyone, let alone a simple steward like myself. Know you also, or so I learnt from one of the notables of the Court, how King Louis is angry. He feels insulted that someone like you should send messages via the hands of a mere commoner.

'Nevertheless, I have talked to those who serve on Louis' council but they have denied me access to the King who has turned Plessis into a veritable fortress. Along the roads leading to it, caltrops have been scattered to bring down the horse of anyone seeking a forced entry. There are also detachments of archers in the forest with orders to kill anyone trespassing near the walls. The King's residence itself is surrounded by a deep ditch and a high wall. The latter has many pronged iron spikes embedded in it. Beyond the wall is a high, iron grille patrolled by sentries. Beyond that, on the four corners of the King's house, are moveable iron watch-towers, each manned by ten crossbow men day and night.

'I merely mention this to show how impossible it is to approach the King or his Court. The French King is absorbed with death, using his vast wealth to fend it off. He has sent presents to the church of St. Martin le Tours and gold chalices to Rome. He has brought a holy man to live in the palace entrusted with the task of interceding constantly wth God on the French King's behalf. I mean no disrespect but Louis has a low opinion of our King. I was surprised to hear, even in France, how rumours about the Princes' death are common gossip, but there is nothing about escape, abduction or the Princes hiding here or anywhere else.

'I am sorry to be the bearer of such bad news but my secret advice is that most people regard the young princes as murdered and our gracious King as their assassin. I only repeat what I have heard and trust you will act on it accordingly. I wish you health and good fortune. I am sending this letter by trusted carrier and when I return will talk to you personally on this matter. God keep you. Thomas Belknap Esquire – 22nd August 1483.'

Belknap's letter proved of little comfort and I kept it amongst my private papers, not daring to show it to the King. Indeed, I secretly chided Belknap in his absence for sealing his letter with sentiments which could be described as treasonable, at a time when treason was common coin. Richard, myself, and the rest of the Court were still waiting for news about Buckingham and it came to us fast. A horseman from London, his mount lathered with sweat, the rider covered in white dust so that he looked like the pale figure of death from the book of the Apocalypse, reached us while we were at Lincoln. He breathlessly informed us how the south had risen in revolt: Kent, Sussex and the West Country. There were many branches but only one root – Buckingham. When Richard heard this, his face became ashen and tight-lipped. He drew his dagger and, time and again, dug the blade into the table-top, gouging it with savage creases.

'Buckingham,' he muttered. 'He who should have been so true.' And, unable to contain his anger any further, he stalked out of the council chamber. Only then did I realise that Richard had not really believed me, Norfolk, or even his own Chancellor. He had deluded himself into believing Buckingham was merely sulking but never treasonable.

Further news deepened the King's anger: the rebels openly proclaimed that Richard had murdered his nephews and, worse, both they and Buckingham publicly rejected him in favour of the Welsh adventurer, Henry Tudor. Richard's rage was terrible to see: eyes blazing, lips curled, his usual pale, sallow complexion flushed with red spots of anger.

Richard had no troops with him so he travelled to
Grantham to assemble them. I commandeered the
spacious, dark-timbered tavern 'The Angel', setting up
the chancery so the King could issue writs and receive
the Great Seal. All the time our spies kept us informed.
We waited for the usual proclamations which might
describe in detail the allegation that Richard had
barbarously murdered his nephews, but, apart from the
usual invective, there was nothing. The King, to bide his
time, retaliated, calling the rebels traitors, adulterers,
bawds. This war of words continued as each side
collected forces. Richard was particularly keen to keep
up clear communications with Norfolk. The Duke's
purpose was to protect the capital and drive a wedge
between the rebels in East Anglia and those to the west
of London.

The weather changed. Rain-clouds, thick and black,
swept over the flat fields of Lincolnshire and the
downpour began. We cursed it then but later thanked
God, for the elements saved our cause. By the middle of
October we had learnt how Buckingham had publicly
unfurled his standard, sending his formal repudiation
of homage to Richard, declaring him a usurper. At the
same time the Duke sent his spies into all the counties,
appealing to the gentry to rise in arms against Richard. I
captured one of these, hanging him from the branch of
an elm tree after ransacking his wallet and pockets for
letters. There were many, all written in the rebellious
Duke's name. I studied them carefully, the rain from
my soaked hair splashing on the letters, turning the
blue/green words to damp splodges. Finally, I threw the
papers away for they told me nothing about the Princes
or provided any clue to their whereabouts, be it in this
life or the next.

I journeyed on to Banbury, hoping to meet up with
Sir John Stonor and others I had summoned to the
King's standard. The levies were to assemble at a

crossroads outside the town and I cursed all the way there for the rain fell in sheets, turning the roads and tracks into muddy rivers which clogged the wheels of our carts and weakened our horses. My men, summoned earlier from South Yorkshire, walked in quiet files, their leather hose and jerkins a soaking mess. Those who had brought arms, breastplates, basinets and other harness, had doffed them into the wagons where leather sheets protected them from rust. At last we reached the agreed meeting-place and waited in the drenching rain for Stonor. A scout was sent out.

He returned in less than an hour to report that a party of horsemen and foot-soldiers were approaching, but he couldn't describe the insignia on their banners. My anxiety about Sir John's loyalty, who had not replied to earlier letters, only grew. I sent the scout back with another man. Only one returned, bloodied and dishevelled, to describe how they had met the outriders, Stonor's men all right, but their banners were Buckingham's.

I asked for their number and despaired when I realised they almost equalled my own. Pulling back my chain-mail coif, the wind-lashed rain beating into my face, I screamed orders, kicking, shoving my men, to turn the carts and wagons into a defensive ring. The soldiers grumbled and swore in their broad flat accents, but we managed to achieve it, men slipping and groaning in the mud, horses neighing and rearing, bucking in their traces. The wagons were emptied, the soldiers drawing bows, quivers, pikes, axes and daggers. My serjeant-at-arms bullied them into some form of battle-line: pikemen just behind the wagons, archers next to the knights, and mounted men-at-arms in the centre of the ring. Stonor's men came on slowly through the driving rain. Armed and helmeted, they resembled spectres out of a nightmare. I espied Stonor, clear in his colours, and cursed him loudly for a traitor. My serjeants took this as a signal. 'Loose!' they shouted and a dark cloud of arrows whirred towards the oncoming force. Most of the arrows fell short. I was glad, I knew Stonor and rather liked him; I had carried the christening robe for one of his children, whilst Anne and his wife, whenever they met, would link arms and go off giggling like two young maids. Now, in the rain and filthy mud of war, all such memories disappeared. I drew my sword, my serjeants rapped out orders, and a second volley of arrows rose up from our circle. Some reached their targets, and two or three of the foot-soldiers fell screaming and kicking in the mire. The enemy line stopped. I climbed onto a wagon and shouted through the rain:

'Stonor, for God's sake put an end to this nonsense! Take your wounded and withdraw!'

I thought he was about to ignore me, but I saw a banner furled and the enemy line fell back. I allowed them to carry their wounded away and we watched their retreat before turning back to join the main force.

Nine

Richard moved his army to Coventry; I found him and his council in good spirits. Norfolk had proved loyal; despite his age and lumbering gait, the Duke had moved swiftly and deadly as any cat. He had sent out reconnoitring parties to occupy Gravesend and the river passages across the Thames, whilst browbeating the citizens to prepare the defences of London. He had despatched a force to Reigate and managed to throw a protective circle around London, vigorously snapping the links between the rebels in Surrey and East Anglia. Sir John Fogge attempted to attack Gravesend but the Duke's men beat them off. Richard now ordered a general advance into the south-west. He proclaimed one thousand pounds reward for Buckingham, dead or alive, and appointed Sir Ralph Assheton as Vice-Constable of England with powers to try all rebels and mete out summary justice. As we advanced south, Assheton took his new office seriously, hanging rebels, even rolling prisoners down hills in barrels with spikes inside. Richard attempted to curb this ferocious enthusiasm but the bloodlust of the royal army was aroused, whetted by the news of Buckingham's revolt being on the wane. The rebel duke had tried to move eastwards from Brecon but he had been constantly harassed by the Vaughan family, chieftains in that area; they cut off his communications with the rest of Wales, attacking the rebel force, even raiding Brecon Castle itself. Elsewhere, his inveterate enemies, the Staffords, systematically wrecked bridges, leaving parties of men to attack Buckingham's force whenever they thought fit.

Richard continued his march into the south-west and we reached Salisbury; the fields and meadows outside the town were soon covered by the silken pavilions of the nobles and the straw-coloured bothies of the common soldiers. The King moved into the city, taking over the episcopal palace of Lionel Woodville; he had supported the rebels but, after Buckingham's revolt collapsed, escaped across the Channel. Belknap rejoined me here, tired and mud-stained after his ride from Dover. I intended to reprove him but changed my mind after one look at his grey, exhausted face.

Later the same evening, both Belknap and myself were aroused by a royal serjeant-at-arms who whispered that the King wished to see me in the Bishop's council chamber. I found Richard excited, his face wreathed in smiles, so pleased he could scarcely stand still but paced up and down the room exclaiming to those members of the secret council who joined him that Buckingham had been taken.

'I do not wish to see him!' he shouted. 'I do not wish to hear that ingrate's voice!' He went up and clapped a hand on Catesby's shoulder. 'William, let Sir Ralph Assheton deal with Buckingham; say I do not wish the Duke's head to be still on his shoulders come Monday morning!' He turned to Ratcliffe: 'Sir Richard, you are to take a convoy of mounted men-at-arms and pursue that episcopal lump, Sir John Morton. Our spies inform us he has fled. He may well escape to the Fens, reach Ely and use his friends and wealth to secure passage abroad.'

'Your Grace!' I turned in surprise to find Belknap behind me. Normally a guard would have barred his entrance but, in the excitement, he had been let through. 'Your Grace,' Belknap repeated. Richard looked questioningly at me.

'Thomas Belknap, your Grace,' I answered. 'My steward.'

'Well,' the King replied. 'What does Thomas Belknap, your steward, wish to say to me?'

'Sire,' Belknap answered coolly, 'I know the Fens well, I once served in Bishop Morton's household. I could be of service to Sir Richard in bringing that old fox to earth.' Richard grinned. He nodded his consent and Belknap, without a by-your-leave, followed Ratcliffe out of the council chamber. At the time, I was not surprised; Belknap's hatred for Morton was as important to him as the fate of the Princes was to me. Devious Belknap, cool and hard. The perfect snake in the grass!

Richard watched them leave before approaching me.

'Buckingham is outside the city!' he hissed. 'I do not wish to see him. You are to go there, Francis. Find out what evils he plotted and who helped him. You will do that?' I agreed, watching Richard's eyes, wondering why the King seemed so relieved at not having to see Buckingham.

The rebellious Duke had been concealed in a tavern just under the castle walls, a dark, dingy place with ragstone walls and blackened wooden beams. The rushes on the floor looked as if they had not been changed for years, the smell was rank, and I glimpsed a dead cat in the far corner. The place was ringed by knights of the royal household in full armour, with more inside; they sat beneath the flickering cresset torches, silent and menacing. In the centre of the room, the reason for their presence, Henry Stafford, Duke of Buckingham, Constable and Grand Chamberlain of England, now adjudged a traitor, was chained and padlocked to a wooden pillar. I had last seen him in his blue and gold gown at Richard's coronation but now his greatness was gone. His clothes were in tatters, his blond hair dirty and bedraggled; his proud face was a mass of bruises and raised welts, the lower lip swollen, one eye half-closed. The captain of the guard stopped me as soon as I entered and, even though he knew me, insisted that I tell him why I had come. Much to my annoyance he searched me for any hidden arms.

'I am sorry, my Lord,' he muttered, 'but the King has authorised this. He is afraid the Duke may seize a knife, despatch himself, and so escape the full rigours of the law.' Once done, the captain let me through. The Duke stirred as he heard me, peering through his one good eye, turning slightly to glimpse me in the poor light.

'Why,' he said, 'it's Lovell the dog! Has the King's cur come to gloat?'

'Not gloat, my Lord,' I said. 'I wish we could have met in more honourable circumstances.' I knelt down, crouching beside him.

'Will the King see me?' Buckingham whispered. I shook my head.

'You will have a priest and, before the day is out, you will appear before Sir Ralph Assheton.' Buckingham's face, despite its horrible bruises, betrayed his fear.

'I am to die?' he said hoarsely.

'Yes, my Lord, you are.'

I could see no point in giving the condemned man false hopes. Buckingham pulled himself up and leaned against the pillar.

'So, what do you want, Lovell?'

'The Princes.'

'Ah!' Buckingham's bloodied mouth opened and, if he could he would have grinned. 'You know the truth, Lovell?' he whispered. 'Oh, I have heard how you were digging amongst the filth in London, but you know, Brackenbury knows, Richard knows, God knows, and soon all the kingdom,' he spat out, 'will realise our usurper is also an assassin!'

'Not necessarily, my Lord,' I replied. 'You were the last to see the Princes alive. I believe you suborned Slaughter and he killed the Princes on your orders.'

Buckingham threw his head back, the laughter cackling in his throat. He coughed and spluttered, a look of pure malevolence in his one good eye.

'Your family emblem is well named, Lovell!' he hissed. 'You are a dog. You follow your master, nose to the ground. I did not kill Slaughter nor did I kill the Princes. I was never party to that. When I saw them in the royal apartments of the Tower, they were alive and in good health.' He lunged forward, his bruised face close against mine. 'Go on, dog! Go and tell your master he is an assassin!' He spat full in my face.

I rose, wiped away the spittle and walked from that hate-filled tavern. Later the same day, on a newly-erected scaffold in the rain-drenched market square of Salisbury, Henry Stafford, Duke of Buckingham, paid for his treason when the town executioner swung his great silver sword, hacking his head from his shoulders.

I did not inform the King about every item of my meeting with Buckingham for I was fascinated by something the Duke had said. According to common rumour, and to the King himself, his Chancellor, Buckingham and, above all, Brackenbury, the Princes had been kept in a small chamber in the White Tower. Buckingham had unwittingly confessed to two things. First he had insisted that the Princes were still in the Tower when he left, so freeing himself from any accusation of abducting them or organising their escape. Secondly, he had said he had last seen the Princes, not in the White Tower but actually in the royal apartments, contrary to what Brackenbury had informed me. I did not realise this contradiction until hours after Buckingham's execution. But, even if I had realised it in time, the Duke, sensing I was interested in such a remark, might only have entangled me deeper in his web of lies.

Another prick to my memory was the confession of Stephen Deverel. He had been a body squire of the

Duke and he gave much information to Assheton in a successful bid to save his own life. I attended these hearings, hoping to trap the spy known as Percivalle, listening carefully to the accents of those taken prisoner with Buckingham – God knows I would never forget that voice. It proved fruitless; none had heard of anyone known as Percivalle, nor could I detect his tones in the different speeches I observed. Deverel's confession, however, was interesting. He reported that he had stayed with the Duke in London and had gone to the Tower with him before the Duke's party journeyed west to meet the King at Gloucester.

In London, Buckingham had attended secret meetings, but Deverel did not know where or with whom. However, on his departure from Gloucester, Buckingham had met up with the Lady Margaret Beaufort, mother of Henry Tudor and wife to Lord Thomas Stanley. She was travelling from London either to visit her estates in the midland counties or some shrine of the Blessed Virgin. They met in a village between Worcester and Bridgenorth, dining alone in an obscure tavern. Buckingham had thought he was safe, not knowing that Deverel, because of the thin walls, could hear a great deal of their conversation. Buckingham confessed to Lady Margaret how he no longer supported Richard, for the King had killed the two Princes. Buckingham insisted he was desirous of better relations between himself and the Countess because of this, as well as his secret talks with his prisoner, Bishop Morton. The Duke admitted that being descended from Thomas of Woodstock, he had entertained hopes of the crown passing to him if Richard was overthrown. Bishop Morton, however, had persuaded him to support the claim of Henry Tudor, promising the Duke that if Richard was removed and Henry came into his own, Buckingham would be amply rewarded.

According to Deverel, the Lady Margaret confirmed Morton's promise. She secured Buckingham's agreement to Henry Tudor's marriage to Elizabeth Woodville's eldest daughter, adding that she would send her own chaplain, Christopher Urswicke, to Brittany to make known Buckingham's intentions. Assheton interrogated Deverel most closely but the man refused to recant. I sat in the crowded Guildhall at Salisbury and believed Deverel was telling the truth, but were others? Did Buckingham, did Brackenbury, and, above all, did Richard my King, know the hidden truth?

Richard was in no mood, however, to be questioned, revelling in his victory over the rebels. Flushed with success, the royal army left Salisbury and swept south to Exeter, a city whose loyalty Richard gravely doubted, calling it a nest of traitors and the hotbed of filthy treason. The city fathers, fearful of the royal wrath, humbly submitted. We found the city gates open, the mayor and leading citizens kneeling in the dust to offer the King the keys to their city. Richard, menacing in his silence, accepted them and led his army into Exeter. The streets were deserted, the market-place empty. We passed the huge, elaborately carved houses of the merchants, surrounded by walled courtyards and sweet-smelling gardens, now drenched after the constant rainfall. Interspaced between them were the modest, square, two-storeyed houses of the artisans working in the cloth trade. All of these, however, looked forsaken, doors and shutters pulled close and tightly fastened. I heard movement behind some; the cry of a child, a shout of anguish, and a brief glimpse of terrified eyes and white faces.

The real object of terror was not so much the King himself but Sir Ralph Assheton, riding alongside him in black plate-armour. Behind the Vice-Constable trundled a huge four-wheeled wagon, painted black and hauled by four great horses, draped in purple, their manes hogged. In the cart was the paraphernalia of Assheton's office; a makeshift gallows, execution block, axe and other instruments of torture. The King led us into the main square of the city, a huge expanse with houses on either side and the large, soaring cathedral at the far end. On a normal day this would be the market area, crowded with people, covered in stalls. Now it was forlorn and deserted except for three figures clad in black with halters around their necks. They knelt on the steps of the cathedral, their hands outstretched, begging for mercy. The King stopped his horse and took off his coronet and helmet. He shook his blood-red hair free and slouched brooding in the saddle at the scene before him. He beckoned me alongside.

'Who are they?' he said, nodding towards the three figures. I spurred my horse across the square, took it up the steps, carefully guiding the horse as its iron-shod hooves clattered and sparked on the hard granite stone. I stared up at the cathedral, the huge steel-studded doors, and above them the tympanum, Christ in full judgement at the end of the world. The three men turned, the first a small, brown-faced man, the other two silver-haired, their white faces glistening with sweat. I stared at them before shouting back:

'I recognise one, Your Grace, as would you: Sir Thomas St. Leger. I do not know the other two.' I knew Sir Thomas well. A crafty man, who thought he would better himself by marrying the King's sister. The King was unmoved by this news; after Buckingham's rebellion he had sworn he would never again be surprised. He leaned over his horse and mumbled a few words to Assheton before standing high in his stirrups, shouting till the square echoed with his words.

'Citizens of Exeter, I forgive you your crimes!' He turned towards the three figures. 'The other two may go, but Sir Thomas, my Lord Vice-Constable must have words with you.' A low moan of terror greeted his words. Sir Thomas bowed lower while his two companions gratefully scampered away.

The King kept his word, the city was spared; but before the day was out Sir Thomas St. Leger was arraigned for treason by Sir Ralph Assheton, found guilty and put to death. That same evening the King ordered me to take troops down to the coast to the small port of Plymouth. His spies had brought news how Henry Tudor, financed with Breton gold, was planning a descent on the coast.

'The Tudor expects,' Richard remarked, 'to be met by Buckingham.' He grinned at me. 'Let us not disappoint him, Francis.'

We camped outside the port and I placed scouts along the cliff. After two days one of these espied a large, three-masted cog, escorted by two caravels which appeared over the horizon. Archers with the keenest sight were despatched to note the colours, and our suspicions were soon confirmed. From the stern of the huge cog hung the pennant of the Red Dragon rampant of Wales.

Of course, the men whom Tudor had expected had long fled. I gave orders for the contents of the two sealed wagons I had brought to be emptied of the captured liveries, standards and pennants of Buckingham. My men dressed in these whilst the huge banner and pennants of the dead Duke were unfurled along the cliff top. The cog hailed into view. On instructions, my men shouted how Buckingham had been successful, loudly inviting Tudor and his escort ashore. My captains and I watched the proceedings. We hid behind fishing-smacks pulled up high on the beach, quietly cursing that no King's ship had appeared to seal off any escape route. I thought Tudor was going to fall into our trap; a small boat was lowered down the side of the cog and I saw four figures tumble in. The boat was rowed quickly ashore but its occupants were four

Breton sailors who became suspicious at the paucity of Buckingham's men and the general air of conspiracy. My men were soldiers, not actors. The sailors were to give a prearranged signal if they were confident there was no trap. Of course they did not; the cog and its escort turned, raised their sails, and I watched despairingly as they made their way out to sea. I ordered the Bretons to be put in chains and we returned dispiritedly to Exeter.

Ten

Richard accepted the Tudor's escape with equanimity, saying there would be other times and other places, before handing me a letter from Anne. As soon as I was alone I broke the seal and read the letter: Anne called me her beloved, saying how, despite the rain, the Minster was still beautiful. My heart skipped a beat, she was enceinte, at least two months gone, and hoped a boy would be born the following summer. The next few sentences made my blood run cold: Anne chattered gaily about a stranger who had appeared at the manor house, well-dressed, softly spoken, with a Welsh accent. He had introduced himself as a long-lost friend called Percivalle and enquired about my whereabouts. He claimed we had recently met and he was anxious to renew our acquaintanceship.

I put the letter away and walked across to a window embrasure overlooking the rain-sodden town, wondering who Percivalle was? Was his arrival at the Minster a personal threat? Yet the fellow appeared to be courteous and offered no harm. Nevertheless, I was frightened; frightened for Anne, for our unborn child and for myself. Richard was wrapped in a web of conspiracy and the collapse of Buckingham's rebellion might only be a brief respite. I re-read the letter; in her few concluding sentences Anne obliquely referred to the evil rumours about the King; once again she was warning me. I had no illusions of what would happen if the King was overthrown. I was his Chamberlain and right-hand man; it would mean the block, the headman's axe and an attainder passed against me and my heirs disinheriting them for life.

I hid my doubts and unease, informing Richard of my good news. The King was pleased, envious, for I knew he wanted more sons to strengthen his new dynasty. He gave me cloths of gold and sent a necklace and a silver dish full of exquisite sweetmeats for Anne. He was still optimistic that Buckingham's rebellion meant the end to all opposition, but fortune was deluding him. Just before we left Exeter four yeomen of the Court were implicated in Buckingham's conspiracy. They had supplied the Duke with privy information and would have escaped undetected had not one of Buckingham's men, an openly declared rebel, bought his life and land by betraying them. They were hanged in the market square. Richard, furious at such treachery, ordered their corpses to be tarred, placed in chains and left as a grim reminder to other would-be rebels.

We marched into East Anglia, linking up with the Duke of Norfolk. The King honoured his premier duke with gratitude and tokens of affection for his loyalty and skill in crushing the rebellion. Outside Gravesend, Richard called a meeting of the secret council, the usual coterie: Kendall, Ratcliffe, Catesby, Brampton, myself and, of course, Norfolk. The King drew up a list of ninety-six rebels whom he wished to attaint in the next Parliament. A fierce debate ensued over what should happen to the ringleaders. The King was for clemency but Catesby argued that the root and cause of the recent revolt, Lady Margaret Beaufort, should be severely punished. I privately agreed with him: Buckingham was not the cause of dissent, there were other more shadowy figures behind him, certainly Morton, Bishop of Ely. The latter had given Ratcliffe and Belknap the slip, escaping into the Fens and taking ship to Flanders.

Belknap had rejoined us as we marched east, quietly confiding to me how he thought Sir Richard Ratcliffe had deliberately allowed Morton to escape. Relations between the two were not cordial; during that council meeting Ratcliffe darkly referred to my arrogant steward as more of an obstacle than a help. However, he refused to elaborate and so I dismissed his remarks as an attempt to pass the blame for Morton's escape on to someone else.

Richard also rejected such comments as petty. He held firm in his determination to show clemency to Lady Margaret Beaufort as it was too dangerous to act otherwise.

'We do not,' he commented, 'want a rift between ourselves and Lady Margaret's husband, Lord Thomas Stanley.' He then murmured, as if talking to himself, 'We will deal with that problem some other time.' Catesby, still hot against Lady Margaret, alleged Beaufort was behind the whispering campaign against Richard, particularly over the fate of the Princes. His words created pools of deep silence.

'Francis.' Richard looked directly at me. 'You are to continue your commission. This matter is not to be dismissed because of Buckingham's death.'

'In which case, your Grace,' I replied, 'I wish words with you afterwards in private.' Richard nodded and the conversation passed on to other matters.

Once the rest had filed out, Richard turned to me, playing with the sparkling gold ring on one of his fingers.

'What is it, Francis?'

'Your Grace, I have two problems,' I replied bluntly. 'Your nephews are gone, perhaps dead. If I am to continue with this matter, I must know why you left Buckingham in London and what happened between you and the Duke at Gloucester?' Richard placed both hands on the table, staring down at me, his lips moving wordlessly. He took deep breaths as if wanting to speak, only to lapse into silence. I just sat and watched, refusing to move until the King had answered my question.

'I am sorry for not telling you earlier, Francis,' he began. 'Before I left London, Buckingham and I had a secret counsel about what should happen to my two nephews.' He chewed at his lower lip. 'True, the possibility of their deaths was discussed but we came to a secret plan. After I left London Buckingham was to enter the Tower and spirit both Princes away.'

'With Brackenbury's knowledge?' I asked.

'No. The only people who knew were myself, Buckingham and my sister Princess Margaret.' I let out a sigh, the King must be telling the truth. Margaret had been his favourite sister, married to the Duke of Burgundy; she would have been only too willing to assist her younger brother. As a boy, Richard saw little of his father or mother. They would arrive with a great train of retainers; hangings would be unpacked, furniture brought in. His parents, dressed gorgeously, would sweep up to talk to him and then they would leave, the Duke and Duchess of York, with their bowmen, men-at-arms, singing boys, trumpeters and servants, clattering across some drawbridge, leaving little Richard to be mothered by Margaret.

'What are you thinking, Francis?' Richard interrupted my thoughts.

I smiled.

'About Margaret. What was she to do?' Richard shrugged.

'She promised she would not harm the boys but find them good homes.'

'But surely,' I replied, 'they would grow up to lay claim to the English crown?'

'Not necessarily so,' Richard replied. 'Their memories would be clouded by comfortable obscurity and who would believe them? They would be well looked after, educated, given every comfort. Perhaps they would not have wished to exchange such comfort for our dangerous world of politics. Moreover,' he added slyly, 'the eldest, Edward, was a very sickly child. I doubt whether he would have lived to manhood.' I agreed. The young prince had been a studious, rather withdrawn boy. There had been times when his parents despaired of him surviving infancy. Indeed, eight years earlier there had been rumours that he had died.

'Do you believe me?' Richard asked.

'It is a preposterous plot,' I replied. 'I mean, it has never happened before.' Richard laughed out loud.

'Oh, yes, it did,' he retorted. 'To my own wife. Surely you remember, Francis?'

Of course I did. Twelve years earlier Richard had planned to marry Anne Neville, only surviving daughter of the Duke of Warwick, but his elder brother, Clarence, had seized her. Richard, hurrying south to claim both her and King Edward's permission for the marriage, went to Clarence's house only to find Anne missing. Clarence boldly insisted he did not know where the woman had gone. Richard, furious, had used all his friends, myself included, to scour London and had eventually discovered the young lady, disguised as a cook-maid, hidden in the kitchens of a friend of Clarence's. The King was correct. It had been done before.

'Who was to take them?' I asked.

'Sir Edward Brampton,' Richard replied. 'He was not given details but simply told to have a ship waiting off the Thames and to take two passengers to Margaret's agents in Ghent. I think Brampton suspected,' Richard added, 'but things went wrong. He waited for his mysterious passengers and, when they failed to arrive, sailed back into port. Buckingham,' he spat out, 'claimed that he had taken the Princes out of the Tower disguised as two of his retainers. He was delayed, so one of his own men took them across to Flanders in another ship, or so he told me at Gloucester.'

'Your Grace,' I replied. 'You should have told me this. And why,' I added angrily, 'did you order me into London to search for the Princes whom you knew were abroad?' Richard brought his hand crashing down onto the table, making me jump.

'I am your King, Viscount Lovell,' Richard shouted. 'I may be your friend but I am also your King. I do not have to make my mind a window for everyone to look through. I was not abusing you,' he said. 'Matters went wrong. First, at Gloucester Buckingham told me the Princes were abroad and I was happy, but then Margaret sent me a secret message saying they had not arrived and my spies reported on the growing rumours that I had killed them. I was confused then and I am now!' He leaned over and grasped me by the wrist. 'Francis, the fate of these boys haunts me. I dare not interrogate Brackenbury,' he sighed deeply. 'I feel I am responsible.'

'Why did you not inform Sir Robert?' I asked.

'Simple,' the King replied. 'The less people knew, the better. In a sense Brackenbury could do nothing. If they went missing from his charge, he would be the last person to proclaim the fact to the world. Moreover, why should I give him such confidences? Men's hearts are fickle, Francis. Why should I entrust such power to Brackenbury?'

'You gave it to Buckingham,' I replied, cursing myself even as I spoke.

'I trusted Buckingham,' he replied evenly. He looked strangely at me. 'I believe my life, Francis, will be ruined because I trusted the wrong people! I tell you this,' he added softly. 'Even on this council, I believe there are men who already have secret pacts with Henry Tudor. If I find them, Francis, even if it is you, I will send them to the axe!'

His words did not concern me, I was loyal. I just hoped he was telling the truth. Poor, secretive Richard. He never trusted anyone, not even me. Oh, he told the truth or rather some of it. The full truth, however, proved more hideous.

Richard entered London at the end of November. He was greeted at the city gates by the mayor and aldermen, dressed in scarlet robes, with five hundred of the principal citizens garbed in violet. They met us at Kennington, escorting us through the cheering crowds in Southwark and across London Bridge to the Wardrobe Palace near Blackfriars. The next day I was with the King; he returned the Great Seal of England in its white, gold-fringed leather bag to the Chancellor and drew up preparations for Christmas and a Parliament in January. I asked permission to return to Minster Lovell but the King reluctantly refused. He took me by the hand and begged me to stay with him, promising he would use all his power to have my wife brought from Minster to Eltham Palace.

Of course I agreed to the King's request. Anne arrived in London a few days before Christmas and we rejoined the court for Yuletide at Eltham in Kent. The setting was memorable enough; the moat, glistening over with ice, spanned by a four-arch bridge, and the great hall, built by Richard's brother, adorned with Turkey cloths and tapestries of gold and silver. Richard insisted that we enjoy ourselves and savour our triumphs after an autumn of hard campaigning. Costly presents were exchanged; Richard gave me a precious set of armour from Milan and Anne a golden egg encrusted with gems. There was dancing, feasting, the cooks not sparing themselves in providing rich sauces, pastries, jellies and blancmanges executed in exquisite designs and shapes. There were masques, mummers' plays, sweet songs and carols from the King's choristers. Richard was determined to lock the world out, though it was present all the time: his wife, now thin and frail, white-faced, her bony body constantly racked by spasms of coughing; and his heir, Edward, conspicuous by his absence, so ill his mother had to leave him at Middleham.

Our spies still reported conspiracies and whisperings in London and Kent as well as news from Brittany. The Tudor had returned safely, openly declaring on oath in Vannes Cathedral that he would take Elizabeth of York as wife, once he had invaded England and overthrown the usurper. This and news that the spy Percivalle was once again busy in the south, spurred Richard into action. Once Twelfth Night was over, preparations were begun for the Parliament called for Friday, January 23rd. On the day before, I kissed Anne goodbye, escorting her and her party of retainers out of the city onto the road north. A hard, cold, bleak day; I held Anne's warm hand in mine, beseeching with my eyes that she take great care of herself and the child growing within her. We had spent the festivities in one whirligig of pleasure. I did not want to question her about Percivalle or the dangers around us. God bless her, I think she knew, but never once did she ask, never once reproach me. As I watched her go, disappearing into the mist, I knew I could face anything but the loss of her.

The King still wished me to pursue the truth behind the fate of the Princes and, though attendant upon him at Court and in Parliament, I used the time to revise what I had learnt.

Item – Richard claimed he had entrusted Buckingham with the task of privily removing the Princes from the Tower and sending them abroad into the care of his sister Margaret, Duchess of Burgundy.

Item – He had not disclosed the plan to Brackenbury but kept it private between himself and Buckingham. He had not since informed Brackenbury because this would achieve nothing.

Item – Buckingham had visited the Tower and claimed

to have seen the Princes in the royal apartments. Brackenbury, however, claimed the meeting took place in the White Tower.

Item – Brackenbury claimed to have seen the Princes the day after Buckingham's visit, so the rebellious duke had not kept to his plan. Sir Edward Brampton had also reported that his expected guests had not boarded the ship as planned. Accordingly, there were a number of conclusions. First, Buckingham could have taken them and Brackenbury could be lying to cover his own mistakes. But why? It would be simple just to accuse Buckingham. Secondly, Buckingham could have taken the Princes, replacing them with boys of similar appearance, but this was too preposterous. Brackenbury would not have hesitated in proclaiming this to the world as well as to the King. Thirdly, Richard could have killed the Princes and Brackenbury could have been his corroborator, but this only led to more questions. Why was the news of the Princes' death rumoured so quickly not only in England but also in France? Why should Richard kill them? This still left other claimants: George, the Duke of Clarence's son, not to mention Edward IV's daughters. The Tudor's proclamation how he intended to marry the eldest of these was sufficient proof that any claimant to the throne could still use Edward IV's children to secure the crown. Moreover, the death of the Princes actually aided the aspirations of any would-be claimant.

There were other problems. Who had killed Slaughter and why? And, if the Princes were dead, how had their bodies been disposed of? The Tower was a small town in itself, it had been a hot summer, the ground would be hard; any attempt to dig graves would soon be noticed. True, the bodies could have been removed by night and dumped in the Thames, but the perpetrators would always run the risk of being noticed or the corpses being discovered. Finally, did Richard have the mind of an assassin? He had executed opponents, but all such deaths had been open. Richard had made no attempt to disguise his own view of justice; Buckingham, Hastings and others had faced secret trials but their executions had been public enough.

Eleven

I teased with these problems for days and, once Parliament was ended, I returned to the Tower on an overcast, fog-bound day. The mists swirled round the mangonels and war-machines lying derelict in the courtyards. The place was active enough, farriers busy seeing to horses before spring and the fires of the smithies blood-red as they obeyed Richard's instructions for new culverins, serpentines, bombards and other cannon. I was allowed access through all the gates but a guard stopped me at the entrance to the royal apartments and insisted on escorting me up to Brackenbury's chamber. The Constable was calmer, more collected, than the last time. He was guarded but at ease. The room was freezing despite the roaring fire and the glittering braziers which had been wheeled into the chamber.

For a few minutes we made desultory conversation. We exchanged civilities and news, discussing common acquaintances at Court and in the recent Parliament, Brackenbury being conspicuous in his absence from both. I studied the man carefully as he chatted, noticing the lines of care around his mouth and deep-set eyes. He knew the rumours. He was Constable of the Tower and the accusation of being a child-murderer does not rest easy, even on the most hardened conscience. Brackenbury sensed my thoughts.

'You are most welcome, my Lord,' he said. 'But you

are here about the Princes. How can I help you this time?'

I told him about my meeting with Buckingham and watched his face pale. He seemed to lose his composure at the dead Duke's claim to have met the Princes not in the White Tower, but here in the royal apartments.

'The man's a liar!' he retorted. 'He saw them in the Tower. I cannot see why the traitor should have made such a comment. There again he was so full of his own pride as well as wine, he would scarcely know he was in London never mind the Tower!'

'And have you learnt anything new, Sir Robert, in the last six months? Any rumour, any whisper?'

'No, nothing.'

I leaned towards him. 'Sir Robert, I am not your enemy or your judge. But for God's sake, man, face the problem. You had custody of the two Princes, yet they disappeared. No one saw them leave. There was no attack. How did they escape? What explanation do you have?'

'I have told you,' he snapped back. 'William Slaughter, he knew his way round the Tower. There are still many secret exits and entrances.'

'Did you know,' I asked slowly, 'that Slaughter is dead?' I held up a hand to fend off his questions. 'I have seen his corpse, throat slit from ear to ear.' Brackenbury's eyes flickered away; he smiled thinly. 'But that is the explanation,' he answered. 'Slaughter took them. He was suborned. He was working for someone else. Once he had carried out their orders ...' Brackenbury shrugged, ' ... Slaughter was of no use, and what he knew was dangerous so he was killed.'

I considered the possibility. Brackenbury was right. The Princes' gaoler could have freed them, but what had then happened to them? Not one sign or hint of their appearance or claim to the throne. Had they been **rescued just to be murdered?**

I left Sir Robert, having gained his permission to question others in the Tower, but I found nothing. All I received were evasive answers, blank looks, even a refusal to answer despite my status as both Richard's Chamberlain and loyal friend. I studied the account for the Tower but discovered nothing, except confirmation that on July 19th the rest of the Princes' retinue had been paid off. There were references to Buckingham's visit but the rest of the items were wages for the garrison and payments to masons and carpenters for the constant building which was carried out in the Tower.

I left the fortress late in the afternoon. I met my retainers outside the main gate and took a barge down to Southwark. As usual, its narrow streets were packed with all the filth of the underworld. Sham beggars, relic-sellers, footpads, whores, pimps, cutpurses, forgers, counterfeiters and murderers. Men who killed another human being for the price of a pot of ale. The stalls and booths were open selling baubles, cheap food or other items, usually stolen from shops across the river. The whores were there but, being so early in the day, acted as discreetly as their painted faces, orange-braided hair and scarlet gowns would allow. We turned down one street where I asked a scribbler for directions to the tavern Sir Edward Brampton constantly frequented. The fellow grinned. Yes, he knew the 'Ragged Staff' and, for a few pennies, sketched directions on a piece of dirty vellum.

One of my retainers, a serjeant-at-arms, led the way. At last we arrived at a huge, three-storeyed building with an ale stake pushed under the eaves and a crude sign above the broad wooden entrance proclaiming it to be the 'Ragged Staff'. Sir Edward Brampton was well-known there. A great navigator from a nation whose sailors are now scouring the dark coasts of Africa, Brampton liked his comforts. Inside it was no different from any other tavern: a large, overheated room, filled with shouting, half-drunk customers seated around stout wooden tables. They were busy baiting a relic-seller, who claimed to be selling hairs from St. Paul's beard. The upper storeys, however, housed a luxurious bordello and I found Brampton there, lying upon a great four-poster bed, on either side of him a giggling wench, almost identical with their black curly hair and gentle curves of pink and white flesh. They lay on lace-fringed covers, a sheer contrast to the dark, swarthy body of Sir Edward. Around the room were strewn silken garments, dresses, petticoats and red hose with golden roses on them.

A grinning, evil-smelling boy ushered me in; I sent him packing back downstairs with strict instructions to look after my retainers. Only when he closed the door behind him did Brampton see me. He sat up roaring with laughter, inviting me to participate in what he called his great banquet on the bed. I declined and said I wished to speak to him alone. He damned me for being as prim as any archdeacon and, slapping both wenches on the backside, told them to grab their robes and get out before he laid about them with his belt. They slipped by me, brushing my shoulders with their silken flesh. Once they were gone, Brampton rose, wrapping a rather dirty sheet about him, and went over to pour two generous cups of wine, proffering one to me. I remember it tasted delicious, white Rhenish, smooth and chilled in snow or ice.

'Well, Lovell!' he roared. 'What do you want?' God knows he knew why I was there. For all his bluntness and foreign ways, Sir Edward was as keen as I to know the truth. Seated now in the cold darkness, I remember that meeting, the wine, the friendship, the sense of common purpose. It warms me against the chill approach of death.

At the time, however, I was suspicious and he had to repeat his question. I began to ask delicately about the

King's instructions to take a ship, stand off the mouth of the Thames and wait for certain passengers to be put aboard. His eyes hardened, shifting away from mine.

'Sir Edward,' I said tiredly, 'you know the King has instructed me in this matter. He has probably asked you what happened and I have his authority to ask the same. When was it?' I asked. 'What time?'

'After dark,' he replied. 'On the evening of July 25th.' The same day, I noted, as Buckingham went to the Tower.

'But no one came?' I asked.

'No one,' he replied. 'We were instructed to take up our position just after dark; it was almost dawn before we raised anchor and sailed away.' I searched his face for any lies but he just shrugged his shoulders, rubbing his ear lobe, playing with the gold pearl-studded ring which dangled from it.

'You know who your intended passengers were?'

'Of course,' Brampton snapped back. 'Richard's bastard nephews.'

'So what do you think happened?'

'The bastard princes?' He sat on the edge of the bed and sipped from his cup. 'They may be dead or they may have escaped. I keep my eyes and ears open. I think they are abroad.'

'What makes you so certain?' I asked.

He put the cup down and leaned across to me.

'Just rumours. Stories from Tournai.' My heart quickened. I wish it had not, for Brampton sowed a seed that day, the seeds of destruction. I pressed him for more details but he could tell me nothing more. He said he had recently informed the King but so far he had found nothing to add.

I left Brampton with his whores and went back downstairs. A strumpet with an orange wig and a red, loose, flowing dress tried to block my way; a young girl with a soft, sweet face and eyes as hard as steel. She whispered promises of delights for a drink or a few coins. I tried to push by her but she blocked my path. The stairs were empty, dark and gloomy, the girl's arm hard against my stomach. I heard the clink of steel behind me, the soft slither of leather on wood, and, suspecting a trap, threw her aside, running down the stairs shouting for my retainers to the shrill mocking laughter of the doxy.

The next morning I was up early and, escorted by a now grumbling group of servants, went up to Holborn and the stately grand town house of Lord Thomas Stanley. I found it easily enough, the largest in the area, more like an inn with its spacious courtyards, orchards and raised flower-beds. The bricks between the jet-black timbers glistened with fresh coats of white paint and the gables were gilted with ornate embosses and small shields bearing the red insignia of the Stanleys. Both courtyard and house were full of retainers and they greeted my arrival with cool disdain. The Stanleys had never been Richard's friends. Lord Thomas had been allied to Hastings and arrested in that frenetic meeting in the Tower. He had been thrown roughly to the ground, banging his head so hard he was led off covered in blood. Stanley never forgave nor forgot either the blow or the accompanying humiliation. Richard had tried to buy him with honours, but the only person Stanley really supported was himself. His family were weasels, time-servers, switching sides to suit their own convenience. Richard was frightened of his great power in the counties of Cheshire and Lancashire but, in hindsight, Richard's greatest mistake was not having him executed.

Stanley's second wife, Lady Margaret Beaufort, was the perfect match for him. She was the sole heir of the Duke of Somerset, one of the House of Lancaster's most powerful generals. She had been married at the age of thirteen to Edmund Tudor, Earl of Richmond; their son Henry was now the only surviving Lancastrian claimant to the throne. By all rights she should have been locked up in prison but Richard, unwilling or unable to confront her new husband, had simply stripped her of her titles, her lands given to her husband who was to be the guarantor of her future good behaviour.

I was not looking forward to the meeting and, as I was ushered upstairs to a small comfortable chamber, found myself strangely nervous. The Lady Margaret was waiting for me, seated in a huge chair before the hearth of a roaring fire. A diminutive woman, she nevertheless had a presence, sitting there in a dark-blue velvet dress, fringed at neck and cuffs with frothy white Bruges lace. She did not wear an elegant Court head-dress but a white veil like a nun's which framed her thin, pale face and large dark eyes, pools of passionate power. She did not stir as I entered except to raise her hand to be kissed before gesturing me to sit in the chair opposite. Like some great abbess she insisted on the civilities, offering me wine and a dish of cloying sweetmeats. She was the most powerful and dangerous woman I have ever met. She exuded a baleful, threatening presence. Her arrogant face and thin lips concealed any disappointment or humiliation she may have felt following Buckingham's defeat and Richard's public rebukes at her involvement.

'Why are you here, my Lord?' she said in a whisper. I stared back, challenging the malicious menace of this diminutive woman and undoubted traitor.

'My Lady,' I replied. 'The Duke of Buckingham's late lamented rebellion. You were involved?'

'So Parliament says,' she quickly replied.

'And you?' I asked. 'What do you say?' She smirked.

'What do I care? More importantly, why do you?'

I decided to end this cat-and-mouse game.

'My Lady, when the King left on his progress through

the shires, you stayed in London?' She nodded. 'And so,' I added, 'did the Duke of Buckingham.'

'So?' One raised eyebrow seemed to dismiss my question as nonsense.

'In that time,' I asked harshly, 'did you and the Duke of Buckingham meet?' She smiled sweetly.

'I need not answer that.'

'No, my Lady, you may not and I will leave. But the King may very well ask your servants.' I was pleased to see a flicker of alarm in her eyes. We both knew that two of her household, Reginald Bray and her chaplain, Christopher Urswicke, were constantly peddling money and information to her son in Brittany.

'You would not dare!' she hissed.

'I would dare, Madame. It is remarkable what people will say after a short sojourn in the dungeons of the Tower. Madame, we are talking about treason. Of plotting with the King's enemies both here and abroad. The King has been clement but his mood could change.'

'Old Dick!' she jibed. 'Little Dickon of Gloucester! How high he has risen!'

'He is the King, Madame,' I replied.

'He is the King,' she mimicked back.

'Madame, if you will not talk to me, then I shall ask to meet Masters Bray and Urswicke in less salubrious surroundings.'

'Sit down, man!' Her voice was still harsh but I detected the note of fear. 'Buckingham,' she began more evenly, 'came to see me once the King had left on his progress through the shires. He informed me how he and other gentlemen were sickened by Richard of Gloucester's seizure of the crown and the destruction of his nephews. He said he wished to change his allegiance and hoped this information would be conveyed to my son, in Brittany.'

'So, Buckingham informed you that the Princes were dead?'

'Yes, he did.'

'On what day was this, Madame?'

'On the evening of July 25th,' she said after a long pause as if trying to recollect. 'He came here, late at night, to tell me the Princes were no more.' I stared at her, trying to conceal my own surprise. Here, indeed, was a riddle. When Buckingham and this lady met, the Princes were alive and well. Indeed, they were seen the following day by Brackenbury. But when Buckingham was falsely informing this lady that the Princes were dead, he knew that Brampton was waiting up the Thames with a ship to take them abroad. What had been Buckingham's game? He seemed to change his message depending on whom he was speaking to. The Lady Margaret leaned across.

'You seem bemused, my Lord?' she asked smugly.

'No,' I lied. 'A little puzzled about how the Duke should know the Princes were dead. Did he give you any evidence for this?'

'Oh, yes,' the Lady Margaret smiled. 'Before the King had left London, he and Buckingham met in secret council at Baynards Castle. There, in a private chamber, your master told Buckingham he had sent secret instructions with Sir James Tyrrell to Brackenbury that the Princes were to be silently removed for the good of the realm. How does it feel, Viscount,' she rasped, 'to be the servant of an assassin? A child-murderer!' I glared back at the woman. She considered Richard a hypocrite but she was no less a Pharisee herself. Three times married, the patroness of religious works and monastic houses, she prided herself on direct communication with God, claiming to have had visions since the age of nine. Strange, isn't it, when we burnt the Maid at Rouen for claiming to have similar dreams and fantasies? The Lady Margaret believed her son was the reincarnation of Arthur, the Welsh prince, who would come out of Wales and wield total power over the realm. People who have visions are dangerous. They tend to think that if God will not help their dreams to be realised, they ought to offer a little help themselves.

However, I run on. I promised to let this story unfold and not to endow it with the virtue of hindsight. At the time, the Lady Margaret seemed composed enough so I decided to press her further.

'My Lady, Buckingham met you here in London and again outside Worcester. Why was it important for two great notables to meet in some dirty tavern in the middle of the countryside?' The Beaufort woman shrugged.

'The meeting was accidental, though I knew Buckingham was in the area. He simply wished to affirm his allegiance and repeat his story how the King had murdered his nephews.'

The Lady Margaret was going to reveal no more. She would continue to lie and mock me, but at least I could shake her calm demeanour. I rose, unceremoniously bowed and, turning on my heel, walked back to the door.

'So, my Lord, did you learn anything fresh?' She could not resist the jibe. I walked back.

'Oh, yes, my Lady,' I answered. 'You see, the night Buckingham came to tell you that the Princes were dead – well, he was lying. On the day after, both boys were seen by Brackenbury.' My heart warmed to see the alarm and panic in her eyes. She clenched her little white fists, her mask of serenity replaced by a look of furious hatred.

'That is a lie!' she snarled. 'The Princes are dead! Your master killed them!'

'Oh no,' I answered casually. 'They may not be dead. I am sure you have your spies, Lady Margaret. Perhaps you know a man called Percivalle? He will inform you about my secret business. Let us say, Lady Margaret,' I taunted further, 'that your son does invade, and let us say my master is overthrown.' I walked nearer, pushing my face close against hers. 'What then, Lady Margaret? Your son is nothing but the misbegotten creation of a lady whose family are debarred from the throne. Whose father and grandfather were nothing better than Welsh adventurers. So, how will he hold his throne? Richard's son still lives. Clarence's son still lives. The daughters of Edward IV still live and, God willing, so do his sons! Remember that next time you have a vision or you plot here in this secret chamber!' I turned and walked away.

'Lovell!' Her voice hissed like a snake behind me. I glanced over my shoulder. Lady Margaret had half risen out of her chair, her face white, drawn with fury, one hand jabbing a finger towards me.

'Lovell,' she whispered, 'I promise you this. I shall never forget you!'

I smiled and sauntered off, but in my heart, for the first time ever, I knew what it was to hate and be hated in return.

Twelve

My meeting with the Beaufort woman rankled so deeply I could not continue with the matter. Instead I returned to Westminster, busying myself with household duties: I checked stores, paid wages, drew up indentures with servants, drafted letters to clerks and organised the despatch of purveyors for the King's journey north again. I had news from Anne, how she was well and wished my speedy return.

'Spring will come soon,' she wrote, 'and I would like you to be here. I was pleased to see Thomas and have full trust in his care and devotion for you.' I kept the letter close to my heart, richly thanked Belknap and despatched him back to Minster Lovell with instructions to see my wife wanted for nothing and had no anxieties. As usual, the loyal, ever-faithful Belknap calmly agreed and quietly left. There was a time when I used to rage against the man but perhaps I am to blame – a poor soldier, so intent on watching the enemy from afar, never looking down to see who is crouching at my feet. I asked the King for permission to withdraw from the Court but again he refused. We walked, arms linked as we had as boys, down an empty, stone-vaulted corridor. He kept repeating how much he needed me, questioning me on the secret matter and confiding that if I had any doubts about his probity, he would soon provide both me and the world with ample proof of his good intentions. I remember stopping, studying him

114

carefully, noting the grey hairs sprinkled amongst the red. How white and pinched his face had become, his eyes constantly flickering as if searching out enemies. Once warm and friendly, they seemed to glitter frenetically as if trying to hide guilt or nagging doubt.

The boy from Middleham Castle had gone and so had the shrewd, patient general in the north. I felt sorry for him.

'Richard,' I asked. 'Is all this worth it? Do you think you did right?' He half turned, looking at me warily from the corner of his eye.

'What answer can I give?' he replied. 'Do you remember, Francis, when we used to hunt? We would flush out a deer and make it run, keeping it within bounds; the creature fled but we were always behind him and there were traps on either side. He could only go forward. Well, that is me. What can, what could I do? Remain the King's uncle? Stay in the north until the Woodvilles invited me to a banquet in London, insisting on sending a thousand lancers to accompany me? And then what? Some treasonable allegation, a secret trial in the Tower and join my brother Clarence, drowned in some vat of wine, or knocked quietly on the head? Is that what we fought for, Francis? At Tewkesbury, at Barnet? Is that why my father and brother lost their heads at Wakefield, just to hand it over? To see it all finished while the Woodvilles banqueted, drank and boasted how they would live and rule for ever? No, Francis, there is only one way we can go and that is forward!'

The King had made a similar speech on previous occasions but never with such passion and fury. At the time it shook me, and again I wondered if Richard thought the lives of two young princes were expendable? But then the King achieved something which, for a while, soothed n.y nagging doubts. In the middle of March, Elizabeth Woodville and her daughters left sanctuary in Westminster Abbey, placing themselves under the King's protection. Richard publicly vowed he would care for the ex-queen and all her daughters. The news was so sudden it took me and the Court by surprise.

The Woodville woman was placed in a very comfortable but isolated manor under the care of Captain John Nesfield, while her daughters were taken to the royal household. They were placed in the care of Richard's queen but, as Chamberlain, I had direct responsibility for them. I decided to use this to continue my investigations, for the Woodvilles' submission puzzled me. Here was a woman whose marriage, family and rights Richard had cruelly usurped. She must have hated Richard. How could such a woman submit to a man she believed had murdered her own offspring?

It would be futile to question the former queen but her daughter was a different matter. I took every opportunity to cultivate Elizabeth's acquaintance and placate any animosity. After a while I won her trust or at least part of it. Elizabeth was quiet, shy, but a very beautiful girl. Long blonde hair, pale skin with a fine sheen of gold and blue eyes, heavy-lidded, with lashes as long and as graceful as the wings of a butterfly. She enjoyed talking about her father's triumphs and zest for life and I knew enough stories to keep her amused. One day, shortly after she rejoined us at the Court, I found her alone, sitting in a window bower singing softly to herself as she stared down at the garden below. The Court was quiet, stunned by the grievous news from the north – Richard's one and only son had died. The boy had been frail, weakened by fits of coughing, sometimes unable to walk. Richard was distraught, not only because he had lost a son but also an heir to inherit his hard-earned conquests. The King, seeing it as God's judgment, withdrew into himself. The gossip-mongers were quick to whisper how God had taken from the

King what the King had taken from his brother. Young Elizabeth, however, was untouched by this news. She kept her own counsel, so I seized the opportunity to question her about her brothers. I sat opposite, teasing her, but she just smiled shyly, fending off my questions. I sat closer.

'Elizabeth?'

'Yes, my Lord?'

'Your brothers, the Princes?' The blue eyes clouded with pain. 'I know,' I hurried on, 'how the subject must hurt you but two things concern me. When I met your mother in sanctuary she must have heard the news. The rumours about her sons' deaths. Nevertheless she remains calm and composed and, a few months later, actually submits to the man whom these rumours name as your brothers' assassin!' I thought the girl was going to break into tears; she bit her lip, twisting her long, white fingers together.

'There is no mystery,' she replied quickly. 'My mother still believes her sons are alive.' Elizabeth looked up earnestly at me. 'And if they are, how can she blame the King?'

'But the rumours?' I insisted.

'Oh,' she said wearily, 'we heard about them but my mother had a visitor, a man called ...'

'Percivalle,' I added.

'Yes.' The princess smiled quickly. 'Percivalle. He told my mother how the Duke of Buckingham had spirited her sons abroad but that in the end all would be well.'

'Does your mother really believe that?'

'Oh, yes. She has even written to my half-brother, the Marquis of Dorset, that he can leave France and come home and make his peace with the King.' I nodded understandingly. I had heard such a tale myself, further vindication of how the Woodvilles, for all their hatred or Richard, might not really believe he had assassinated the young Princes. I could see the subject was distressing her so I deftly turned the conversation onto other, lighter topics. Nevertheless what she told me confirmed my earlier suspicions; Buckingham had only been too willing to tell his listeners what they wanted to hear.

The ubiquitous Percivalle was another matter. I sent a hasty memorandum to the council demanding that all the powers of the Crown should be used in trapping this constant troublemaker. The King agreed, though, asserting himself after his son's death, he was more involved in driving the Scots off the northern seas and securing a truce with the vacillating James III of Scotland. Richard was still subdued, shocked by his son's death but elated at how the Woodvilles had come to accept him. Henry Tudor in Brittany was another matter. Our spies had reported how Duke Francis of Brittany had suffered some form of mental collapse brought on by evil humours of the brain. His chancellor Pierre Landois, more amicable to Richard, now insisted the Tudor Pretender should be kept in close confinement. Richard sent huge bribes to Landois and a secret emissary to ensure that the chancellor kept his word. At my request Thomas Belknap was one of these envoys. He had additional instructions to proceed from Brittany to Margaret of Burgundy to enquire if there were any truth in the rumours reported to him by Sir Edward Brampton.

The King also had secret instructions for me.

'Francis,' he remarked dourly. 'We have had little joy in finding the whereabouts of the two Princes. I myself have spoken to Brackenbury and cannot make any sense out of the man. If we cannot find the truth, we can at least crush the rumours that I was their murderer. There has been no trace of my brother's sons. nor has anyone pretending to be them come forward. The intelligence from foreign Courts is similar.' He looked sharply at me. 'I believe poor Brampton's rumours are more the result of wishful thinking than hard facts.' He paused, rubbing his fingers across his lips. 'I have read your memorandum about Percivalle. I agree. It is time we tracked him down.' He clapped me on the shoulder. 'Francis, let it be known that your loyalty to me is not what it should be. Perhaps we can then flush this Percivalle out into the open.'

At first I did not agree with the King, relying more on spies, rumours, whispers, in searching Percivalle out. Yet each time our nets dragged nothing out. In the middle of July, an act of gross impunity made the hunt more frenetic. Percivalle, or so I understood later, composed a doggerel. He distributed it around London, even copying it on a placard which he nailed to the door of St. Paul's Cathedral. A rhyming couplet, it soon caught the imagination and tickled the humour of the Londoners:

'The Rat, the Cat and Lovell the Dog,
Rules all England under the Hog.'

The King was furious but I admired the ingenuity of its composer. It was a catchy, jingly phrase; a contemptuous attack upon Richard, his personal emblem of the White Boar, Sir Richard Ratcliffe, William Catesby and, of course, myself.

The King's council met in secret session; Richard furiously demanded what progress I had made in searching out Percivalle. He sarcastically derided me as futile, glowering at me as if I was to blame. I argued back just as fiercely, saying that in this matter, as with the fate of the Princes, I was just floundering in the dark. Nevertheless, I acted on his advice, I sent an anonymous letter to Lady Margaret Beaufort for I knew she lay at the centre of this web of intrigue. The message, unsigned, simply related how Viscount Lovell now believed the Duke of Buckingham was right. I thought the ruse would work but it failed. The only answer I received was a scrap of parchment nailed to my own door with the words 'Not even a dog bites the hand which feeds it'. My success in capturing Percivalle was more due to sheer chance than any guile. The King sent me on a mission, as personal envoy to his mother, Cecily, who lived as a virtual recluse in her own apartments at Berkhamstead Castle. The Queen Mother, once so beautiful she was called the Rose of Raby, was now a white-haired, austere old woman with her mind more on spiritual matters than those of this world. Relations between her and Richard had always been very cool. The King had confided to me years earlier how this was due to his birth being a most difficult one. Princess Cecily was cordial enough to me; accepting her son's letters but not bothering to open them, she continued her polite conversation. At length, exhausted by this, I rose and gratefully withdrew. I was hungry and rather thirsty and went down to the buttery for victuals and a pot of ale. The wood-panelled room was thronged with retainers and servants and, like a bell sounding through a mist, I heard that sing-song accent I had last heard in my chamber in Crosby Place. The voice died away and though I searched the room, I could not trace the speaker. Nonetheless, elated at my discovery, I hastened back to London, secured troops, and returned to Berkhamstead Castle.

Perhaps my lack of interest in the buttery had soothed the anxieties of this most secretive of spies for, once the castle was thronged with soldiers, I learnt that no one had left. I seated myself in the great hall beneath its smoke-blackened timber beams, and questioned each of Princess Cecily's retainers. The process was long and exhausting. I had the Queen Mother's steward sitting alongside to ensure no one staged any pretence and eventually I had trapped my quarry, a young fellow, perhaps in his early thirties, with tousled black hair and an open frank face. He introduced himself as William Collingbourne, a gentleman from Wiltshire, and of Princess Cecily's household. He had the effrontery to think he would escape. I formally arrested him, loading him with chains to take him back to London, and his cool demeanour began to crumble.

I ignored the due process of the law and swiftly transported him to one of the dankest cells at Newgate. There the questioning began, first by me, afterwards by those more skilled in wrenching out the truth – dark, shadowy men who lived in the twilight of the law, garbed completely in black, their faces hidden by red masks. They tortured Collingbourne. He broke and confessed, admitting he was a loyal adherent of both the Tudor in Brittany and the late, but not lamented, Duke of Buckingham. He confessed he was the Tudor's agent, sending him information about the King's defences both on land and at sea, as well as being the author of the doggerel rhyme pinned to the door of St. Paul's Cathedral. Once news of his confession had reached me, I insisted on questioning him myself and went up into West Chepe to the sombre, stark buildings of Newgate prison. These are no more than a collection of towers and tenements built into the old city wall. A pest-ridden place, as on its far side was the city ditch, the open latrine and cesspit of London.

Richard Scarisbrooke, royal serjeant and Constable of the King's prison, insisted on greeting me himself. A frightening sight. Tall, angular, dressed in a dirty red gown tied loosely round the middle, he tried to ape the manners of a courtier. His lean, sallow face with its deep-set eyes and mouth tight as a purse, was covered in small black warts, but his yellow hair was crimped and curled like a boy's. He stood like Satan with his minions around him, a collection of rogues dressed in black rags and leather aprons. They escorted me in mock solemnity through the prison courtyard to Collingbourne's cell, a stone cavern, with wet mildewed walls and rotting black straw, with rays of light let in through the cracks and seams of a heavy trapdoor. A diabolical place, I describe it, yet I have found there are more terrifying prisons to die in than Newgate.

Scarisbrooke lifted the heavy trapdoor and lowered a ladder for me to go down. I was not frightened of Collingbourne – he lay in a pile of wet straw in the corner manacled by chains to the wall whilst I was armed with sword and dagger. God have mercy, I pitied him. He was a dreadful sight. Clothed in rags, his body seemed to be a mass of wounds, his eyes half-closed with bruises, the blood still seeping through smashed teeth and swollen lips. He may have been broken but there was still a spark of defiance in his eyes.

'Viscount Lovell,' he grated. 'Welcome to my humble abode.' He raised a chained hand. 'If I could, I would make you more comfortable.' I turned and bellowed to Scarisbrooke, standing above me, to throw down a bottle of wine and a rag. These he did, and, crouching close to Collingbourne, I bathed his lips with the wine before raising the leather pannikin to squeeze some into his mouth. He thanked me with a look before falling back against the wall.

'Master Collingbourne,' I said. 'Or shall I call you Percivalle? I am sorry to see any man in this state. Even one who has tried to assassinate me at least twice.' Percivalle, his mouth slack, shook his head and muttered something. 'What was that?' I asked.

'Never once,' he said. 'Never once did I attempt to kill you.' I knew he was telling the truth and I briefly wondered who was behind the attempts outside the Tower and in the tavern after I had met Brampton.

'That may be so,' I replied. 'But you know why I am here. Not your links with the Tudor but the fate of the Princes. Different stories circulate,' I said quietly. 'They are murdered. They have disappeared. They have been taken abroad. In God's name, Collingbourne, before you die, tell me the truth!' The prisoner just looked at me. 'Did you know William Slaughter?' I asked. 'Black Will, a gaoler from the Tower?' Collingbourne shook his head. 'Who then,' I insisted, 'told you about the Princes?'

'Buckingham,' he replied. 'I met him,' he licked his bloodied lips, 'I forget the day, some time at the end of July. I met him in his London house. Proud as a peacock he was, nervous but excited. He gave me two messages. The first was the Princes were dead; I was to circulate this news around the city. The second was that the Princes had escaped. I was to take that information to the Woodville woman in Westminster Abbey.'

'You did not ask Buckingham to explain the contradiction?' I asked. Something close to a grin flitted across Collingbourne's face.

'Who cares, Viscount Lovell? Who cares? Buckingham? Richard? The Princes? They do not concern me. The rightful claimant now hides in Brittany, but, like Arthur of old, he will come again.'

'Tell me one final thing,' I asked. 'Was all this Buckingham's work?' Collingbourne laughed, his bruised chest racked with sobs.

'Buckingham,' he gasped, 'was a peacock. He had a brain and tongue like quicksilver but others manipulated him.'

'Who?'

'I do not know. They worked in the shadows as Buckingham and I did. Buckingham concealed himself under friendship to Richard; I thought no one would suspect a retainer working in the Queen Mother's household.' He shrugged. 'You cannot be too confident, my Lord. And you should remember that!'

Thirteen

I left Collingbourne in his wretched prison and returned to the palace at Westminster. A letter was waiting for me from Anne. I had expected it for weeks and knew, as I cut the purple ribbon, it must contain some bad news. Oh, she was well, enjoying the full beautiful summer, the green fields and cool trees of Oxfordshire. All was well, but the child, born late, had died after two days, quietly in its sleep. She prattled on about other news but I knew Anne was trying to control and conceal her searing pain of loss and desolation. I just stood there in the window embrasure looking down at the rose gardens of Westminster Palace, the tears streaming down my cheeks, unable to express the deep, sobbing cries I felt within me.

There was other dismal news to echo my own. The King's plan to seize Henry Tudor had gone amiss. Someone had warned him so Henry had sent letters to Charles VIII of France asking him for sanctuary. Once this was granted, the Tudor acted quickly. A group of supporters under his uncle, Jasper Tudor, left Vannes ostensibly as envoys riding to consult with Duke Francis who still lay ill in a castle near the French border. They then abruptly changed direction, riding directly into Anjou and a warm welcome from the French. Two days later, Henry Tudor and a small party left Vannes on the pretence of visiting friends. Once free of the city, he hid in a wood, quickly changed clothes with a servant and rode hard for the French border. They reached it only a few minutes before troops sent by Chancellor Landois also arrived. Duke Francis of Brittany recovered, publicly upbraiding his chancellor and allowed the rest of the English exiles to join their master in Paris.

The news from Anne, as well as that from France, threw me into a deep fit of depression. Two days later, having despatched a quick letter to the King, I and a small party of servants rode back to Minster Lovell. I stopped caring about the King, about Henry Tudor, about the stinking city and its seething hotbeds of conspiracy. I wanted to be free of it. I am not a religious man. I am a member of the Guild of Holy Trinity. I have built chantries, had Masses said and given grants of land and money to a number of religious houses. I know there is a heaven and a hell and above them Christ sits in judgement. On my ride back to Minster Lovell, these thoughts began to trouble me. Were Richard and all those around him cursed by God? The King had lost his son, his wife was dying and, whilst the Tudor danced and feasted in France, Richard could trust no man. His own mother was alienated from him, Buckingham and others had risen in rebellion. Was it because of what Richard had done? God's punishment on Cain the murderer? And was I to be included in this? My wife weak, torn by grief. My first-born son, a pathetic little bundle buried in the cold darkness of Minster Lovell church.

When I reached the Minster, my black mood of depression had deepened. Anne, pale-faced, her eyes red-rimmed with weeping, did nothing to allay my evil humours. Her show of gaiety was forced. After she greeted me in our chamber, she just crumbled like a wet rag onto the bed, her body shaking with sobs of anguish. I sat beside her, stroking her long black hair. Over near the wall, a small wooden cot which should have held my son now stood empty, a grim reminder of our loss and deprivation.

God knows I tried to comfort her but for weeks she was withdrawn, suffering a deep melancholy of the spirit. I called a physician but his remedies of fennel, hart's tongue, sugar and white wine did little to help Anne's condition. I dismissed him, feeding her myself on eggs beaten into milk. I insisted she walk with me every day in the gardens and the small pleasaunce we had built there. The year drew in, days and nights turned colder. In the evenings we would stay before the great fire, playing Primero, Hazard, or other games of chance. Slowly she recovered, but a harder, more thoughtful Anne emerged and, God forgive me, the canker was placed in the rose. At first, just comments, observations, but Anne began to take great interest in the affairs of the Court and my involvement in them. She gently reminded me of the darker side of Richard's character. The bloodlust after Tewkesbury when the Lancastrian generals had taken sanctuary in the abbey there, only to be dragged out by King Edward and his brother Richard to face summary trial and execution; Richard's ability to act, dissimulate, to be loyal to his friends but ruthless to any who opposed him.

Anne constantly talked about the fate of the Princes. Where were they, she would ask? What had happened? They were in Richard's hands. Bastards or not, they were still his brother's sons, his own nephews. What man could kill young boys, having snatched them from their mother? I saw the storm-clouds gathering. I argued back, demonstrating how it was Buckingham who had insisted that the Princes be placed in the Tower, that Richard had no choice but to take the throne. The boys might well have been illegitimate, and whether they were or not the Woodvilles would have used them to destroy both him and me. Anne angrily brushed such observations aside.

Late one October evening, the trees outside being

stripped of their dying leaves by a cold, howling wind which lashed the mullioned windows with raindrops, Anne stated her accusations.

'Your master,' she hissed, 'is no more than an assassin!' She saw the look of anger in my eyes and came to crouch by me, putting her head in my lap. I stroked her slowly, sadly. The sight of grey in her once jet-black hair soothed my anger, resolving me to let her speak.

'Francis,' she whispered. 'Can't you see God's judgement is against Richard? His own son gone, his wife dying, his enemies both at home and abroad waxing stronger by the day. And we, Francis, we are caught up in the same trap. God is judging us.' She looked up sharply at me. 'I know what you are involved in, Francis. I know the King's secret matter. I have listened to you talk to Belknap, heard the rumours. Francis, we must do something. Distance yourself! Take careful counsel, for if Richard falls, and I believe God will drag him down, must we go with him?' I tried to calm her, reason with her, point out my friendship for the King, his good service to me, the titles, the lands, the bestowal of the Order of the Garter, but she would not listen and a gulf grew up between us.

At night we both lay silently together. At first I rejected totally what Anne had said, but the doubts began to grow. God appeared to have turned his face away from me. I had heard about the new theories coming from Italy and France claiming there was no opposition to a King when what he wanted had force of law. Had Richard thought about that when the order was issued for his nephews to die? I could imagine Catesby, a clever lawyer, silver-tongued, the devil's advocate, succinctly arguing how the crown of England was worth two lives. After all, had not thousands died in the bitter civil war? What were two lives when weighed against the common good? Two secret executions were not too high a price to pay for peace and strong government. If so,

Richard had been using me, a pretext to cover his own guileful ways.

The doubts hardened into certainties. Belknap returned from across the seas, tired and exhausted. He vehemently denied there were any rumours, stories or legends about the Princes' possible survival in the dowager lands of Margaret of Burgundy. I was pleased at his return, his calm, assured ways. His quiet jokes which made Anne laugh. His shrewd subtle hints, how he believed Henry Tudor would soon invade, possibly next spring. And, looking at me, he said it would be wise if we all took careful stock of the situation.

Of course Richard sent letters to me, begging my return to Court. I listened to how the King, under a golden canopy at Nottingham Castle, had formally accepted James III's offer of peace. How the King's rule was growing stronger; lawlessness was curbed, the seas and highways made safer for travellers, the dispensing of justice more rigorous and exact. I described this to Anne and Belknap who had slowly insinuated himself into our conversations. They just ridiculed the news. Belknap declared how horse-dung may make a rose smell sweeter but it still remains horse-shit. This time I did not argue but turned away, leaving Belknap and Anne together discussing some matter or other. At the beginning of November, just after All Hallows, William Catesby arrived at Minster Lovell, bearing a letter from the King. Oh, no request or pretty plea, but a cold formal letter: I present myself in London by the end of the month to be one of the judges at the trial in the Guildhall of William Collingbourne, accused of high treason.

I took Catesby, that secretive man of strange counsel, into the buttery. I served him myself while asking how things were.

'They go well,' he replied smoothly. 'But we miss you, Francis. The King is hurt by your absence, angry that you have left the secret matter.' He looked at me out of the corner of his eyes. 'Francis, we have all risen high, you included. You should not forget that. You have made enemies, Francis. They say you are ungrateful. Others whisper the word "treason".' I seized both his wrists until I saw the pain in his eyes.

'Master Catesby,' I said hoarsely, 'I am the King's true man.' The lawyer smiled but his eyes were hard, uncowed.

'I believe you are, Francis,' he answered. 'But we both know what is coming. Winter will pass, the storms abate and the Tudor will sail from France. You have heard the news?' I shook my head. 'John de Vere, Earl of Oxford; he has escaped and now feasts with the Tudor in the silken palaces of Paris.'

Even I, distanced as I was from Richard, knew this was dreadful news. John de Vere, Earl of Oxford! A die-hard Lancastrian, and their most capable general, the only one Edward IV had ever feared. Thirteen years ago he had commanded the Lancastrian right wing at the battle of Barnet. I remember being there on the slopes of that long hill ten miles north from London. The evening before Easter Sunday, but the weather was cold. A dense sea-mist rolled in covering the valleys, shrouding everything in a deathly silence broken only by the men-at-arms in their iron harness and the archers in padded leather jackets. There was no sun, no moon, just this deep fog which hid noise and made our armour icy and clammy to touch. The battle began hours before dawn. A vicious, bloody fight, hard to distinguish friend from foe. Richard and I were on the right wing, trying to turn the Lancastrian left so as to swing behind them. The battle was nearly lost; on our far left John de Vere, Earl of Oxford, rolled up Hastings' men, the impetus of their charge carrying them south towards Barnet before Oxford regained control and led them back.

Oxford had hoped to take our force in the rear but, in the mist and confusion, he collided with his own men under Montague. Montague's soldiers mistook Oxford's banner of a star with streamers for the Yorkist emblem of a blazing sun and immediately poured a volley of arrows into them. Oxford's force retreated and, suspecting betrayal, they fled, shouting 'Treason! Treason!' And the battle was over. If de Vere had had better luck, the fight could have gone differently. The earl was later captured and placed in Hammes Castle in the English-held land around Calais. Now he had escaped and was with the Tudor. The devil had broken his bonds and, if Tudor did not come back, Oxford certainly would to avenge past defeats and humiliations.

Catesby watched me digest this news as if I was eating a strange meal.

'The King needs you, Francis,' he said quietly. He leaned across the table. 'Whatever you may think, Francis, remember Collingbourne's couplet – you and I are indistinguishable from the King. If he falls, so do we.' Catesby waved a hand and tried to encompass the whole of Minster Lovell. 'All this will go.' I stared at him. Whatever Catesby was, God rest his soul, he was accurate. Five days later I left Minster Lovell. Anne watched me go, her face hard, her eyes unsmiling, no hand raised in friendly farewell. Despite the treacherous roads and continuous downpour I was back in London in two days. The narrow, shit-strewn streets, the huddled houses, the merchants in the Chepe, the midden-heaps, the glorious banners of gold and purple, orange and red, the sound of trumpet and the clink of harness in the street.

I was welcomed rather coolly, Howard, Ratcliffe and others of their ilk clasping my hand while their eyes slid away as if they still liked me but did not know whether to trust me. On November 29th, dressed in my scarlet, ermine-lined robe, I joined the Chief Justice and other judges of the King's Bench, together with Norfolk and other earls, to try Collingbourne. This did not take place before the great marble bench of the King's Court at Westminster but in the great cavernous Guildhall, as if the King wanted Londoners to see justice done. We judges sat high, behind a green-baize table on the broad dais at the far end of the Guildhall. On either side of us tables for the secretaries, scribes, clerks and lawyers. Collingbourne was brought before the bar. He looked pale, dishevelled, tired, but the torture had stopped and some effort had been made to tidy him up for his appearance in court. He rested almost nonchalantly on the bar, the great beamed rail which separated him from the dais, coolly inspecting each of us. When he saw me sitting at the far end, he smiled lazily, as if we were two friends meeting before a stall in Cheapside or a tavern in Southwark.

The trial was a foregone conclusion; Collingbourne refused to acknowledge Richard as King and therefore rejected us as his rightful judges. He called Richard a usurper, boldly confessed to sending letters and money to Henry Tudor in Brittany and offered no apology or defence. The sentence was delivered in the slow, sepulchral tones of the Lord Chief Justice, that William Collingbourne, being adjudged a traitor to the King, be dragged to a place of execution, that he be hanged, cut down whilst still alive, his body opened, his entrails hacked out, before the decapitation and the quartering of his body. The same was to be displayed on London Bridge as a warning to all other enemies of the King both here and abroad.

As a judge I was present when Collingbourne was dragged on a cheap wooden hurdle through the cobbled streets of London to Tower Hill. A cold filthy day; the hurdle rattled over the cobbles, the stones beneath cutting the poor man's back, making him wince and cry out with pain. On Tower Hill a new scaffold had been specially erected. Collingbourne was hoisted up on the back of the same horse which had dragged him through the streets. A noose was put round his neck, the gory and muddied body being allowed to hang for a short while before being cut down and tossed on a great blood-soaked table. The executioner ripped open his belly with a large knife, plucking out his entrails which he burnt on a fire alongside. Collingbourne's screams were terrible to hear. A scene from the depths of hell: the scaffold, the table and executioner black against the lowering sky, the blood pouring in rivers down the table, Collingbourne shrieking, the stench and the orange-tongued fire roaring up as if asking for more. I turned away as the executioner put his hand back into Collingbourne's body.

'Oh, Lord Jesus!' Collingbourne screamed. 'Yet more trouble!' and died as I, crouching down, vomited the goblet of wine I had drunk earlier to stiffen my resolve. God rest Collingbourne. An undoubted traitor but a witty and brave man. He deserved a better death.

I stayed for a number of days in Westminster. Richard came to see me. He was dressed completely in black with a small purple cap displaying the silver badge of the boar. He looked careworn, his face tight and drawn with tension and anxiety. We spoke awhile, Richard begging me with his eyes for a return to our old friendship, but I could not give it. So he smiled, a lopsided grin on his thin sallow face, and patting me gently on the arm, walked away without a backward glance. God knows I think he wanted to say something, take me into his confidence, but he must have seen the pain in my eyes. Roses when they rot smell as sour as any dank weeds. So it is with the wine of friendship; it can curdle to the most bitter vinegar.

Perhaps I should have left for I had another visitor, someone I least expected, forgotten like a meal eaten and never remembered. Yet I wished she had not come for she only hastened the spread of the canker. One of the palace bailiffs, I forget his name, hastened up to tell me how a young maid sought an audience. On any other occasion, he blustered, he would have turned her away, but she had come to the palace many times before whilst I was hiding away in Oxfordshire. She said she had news, for my ears only, about a person of common acquaintance. I reluctantly agreed to see her in a small whitewashed chamber near the Great Hall.

I hardly recognised the girl when she entered, but she kept repeating her name and where we had last met. I remembered her then, from the tavern, the sweetheart of William Slaughter, the Princes' dead gaoler.

'What is it you want?' I asked peevishly, for I had made a quiet resolve not to speak further on the King's secret matter.

'I have a description,' she replied hastily, frightened of my anger.

'Of whom?'

'Of the man last seen with Black Will drinking in a tavern.'

'Give it to me,' I said tiredly, half wishing the girl was gone. She described what she had learnt, haltingly at first but more confidently as she spoke. My tiredness dropped away like a cloak. I made her repeat the description time and again until I knew it was correct. I gave her a small purse of silver and swore her to silence before she left. For a while I just sat, head in hands, one part of me wishing to run out and confront the man she had described, but I knew I would get no truth from him. Sir Robert Brackenbury, Constable of the Tower, would never admit to being the last person seen drinking with the gaoler of the banished princes. He would angrily rebut any claim to lay the man's death at his door. Such a confidence must be kept secret. I would have to wait for better and fairer times. For why should Brackenbury kill a common servant? What did the fellow know which was so dangerous? If Brackenbury killed Slaughter, he must have executed the Princes, and he would only have done that on Richard's orders.

Fourteen

I left Westminster the following day and journeyed back to Minster Lovell. Anne greeted me frostily. I saw Belknap standing behind her and resented the way he flitted from room to room like some silent shadow. Nonetheless, when I poured my heart out to her, entrusting her with my suspicions about the King and the possible fate of the Princes, Anne's icy demeanour began to thaw. I saw the old glint of merriment dance back into her eyes. She hugged me like she did, oh so long ago, before I became lost in the marshes of the King's tortuous mind. Richard, of course, sent me invitations to join him for Christmas at Westminster but I replied that I was ill, unable to travel. I left him to his own devices. The rumours, of course, came through, of how the King hid his cares under the mantle of splendid celebrations. The shops in Cheapside were full of silver goods and the choirs from London churches serenaded the gentry and merchants with festive carols. In the palace itself there were masques, mummers' plays, dancing and gorgeous banquets. Yet I was glad I was not there. Indeed, I still am, for Anne and I drank the loving-cup, hunted, danced, feasted and surprised each other with presents. We decorated the hall with greenery, hiring troupes of minstrels and mummers. Children from the village came up to entertain us with their songs and dances. A splendid Christmas. A time for wining and eating, of enjoyment during the day and warm silken passion at night. I am glad. It was the last Christmas Anne and I were ever to spend together.

After Twelfth Night, teasing and cajoling Anne, I put an end to the festivities. I insisted we both concentrate on the administration of our estates, not only around Minster but those held in other shires. I summoned bailiffs, reeves, tenants and other members of my retinue to present their accounts, instructing Belknap to take careful measures to ensure our new-found wealth was not wasted. Of course, I kept an ear cocked for any news from Westminster. We had our visitors, Catesby, Ratcliffe, and on one occasion, Howard himself, the Duke of Norfolk cantering up into our main courtyard, filling it with noise and the blue and gold colours of his retinue. The news was always the same. Richard crouched in Westminster, melancholic and sad. Like King Saul from the Old Testament, he felt rejected by God, waiting for the sword to fall on his house. His queen was dying, taken to her bed, her thin body wasting away, coughing her lungs out in short, sharp, bloody gasps. The physicians would not allow Richard anywhere near her and so the rumours had begun, how the King was poisoning his wife. Richard howled like a cornered wolf, cursing God for taking his son and now his own wife in a long-drawn-out death agony of pain. March came. The winds howled in over the country and news arrived that Queen Anne had at last died at Westminster. Outside, Londoners stared and marvelled at the great shadow which crossed the sun. They took this and the Queen's death as an omen that heaven had deserted the House of York.

There was other news. Charles VIII of France had agreed to finance Henry Tudor with money, men and ships. Rumour had it that once spring came the banners of the Red Dragon would be seen again in England. Richard stirred himself. He sent letters begging my return. I was sorely tempted to reply but remembered

Brackenbury's closed face and wondered if Richard had been secretly laughing at me all the time. Catesby returned one evening, claiming he had been sent by Richard. Once Anne heard of his arrival, she withdrew to her own chamber saying she would have nothing to do with the King's cat. Catesby's face told me all, worried, tense and fearful. He gave the gossip of the court, gulping noisily from his cup as if he wished such matters out of the way. I just sat opposite him, relaxed, listening to the man's chatter and through him Richard's pleas that I return to court. After a while Catesby lapsed into silence. He rubbed the wine-cup between his hands, biting his lip, looking down at the floor like the clever lawyer he was, preparing his words carefully. At last he got up and walked over to the dresser to fill his wine-cup. He checked that both doors and windows were locked fast and secure and, dragging his chair over, crouched like a conspirator beside me.

'The Tudor will come!' he said. He stopped and flickered his eyes nervously at me. 'The Tudor will come!' he repeated. Still I remained silent. 'For God's sake, Francis,' he hissed, 'Richard is finished! The Stanleys hate him. The Beaufort bitch plots against him. The Earl of Northumberland detests him for taking away his power in the north. And who is there left? Jack of Norfolk?' Catesby gulped from the cup. 'Old Jack, sixty years old. And our King? He has no heir, not even a wife. Do you know, he has to nominate his own nephew as a possible heir-apparent?' Catesby snorted with laughter. 'Do you really think we would allow the crown to go to John de la Pole? He may be the Earl of Lincoln but his ancestors were merchants from Hull. And the Tudor? He has Oxford, an army, French gold and French ships. Francis, what will happen to us?' I stared back at him. 'What will happen to you, Francis? To Anne?' Then, echoing Belknap's words, 'A careful man, Francis, plans for the future.'

'What are your plans, William?' I asked. 'What do you suggest? Shall we ape Buckingham? Invite the Tudor over, to be caught, trapped in some river valley while our troops desert us? Richard furious, more work for Sir Ralph Assheton, and finally some market square, our heads hacked off for the amusement of gawking rustics. Is that what you want, William? Our King may well survive. If we deserted him, I know Richard, and he would have no mercy.' Catesby nervously wiped his mouth with the back of his hand.

'But if God is against us,' he replied, 'Richard will be defeated.'

'What makes you think God has taken sides?' I asked.

'Richard thinks so himself,' Catesby answered. 'Last August he had the corpse of Henry VI exhumed from its thirteen-year-old resting-place in Chertsey Abbey and reinterred in St. George's Chapel in Windsor. Richard has turned it into a shrine and no wonder – the dead King's corpse was pleasantly scented, uncorrupted, the face as it was on the day of burial, except a little sunken and emaciated.' Catesby shook himself as if trying to drive away an evil phantasm. 'Richard sees all this as signs that God has left him. He cannot sleep at night and insists on paying for thousands of Masses for all members of his family. He gives vestments to York Minster and plans to install a massive chancery there with six altars and a hundred priests. The cost will be enormous. It means Mass will be celebrated incessantly without any break.' Catesby looked down at his hands and I noticed they were trembling slightly. 'I once asked Richard,' the lawyer continued, 'was he trying to buy himself into heaven? The King just stared at me and answered, I think before he could recollect, "I do it, William, in part satisfaction for those things which, on the dreadful day of judgement, I shall answer for".' Catesby looked at me. 'What things, Francis? What dreadful things have been done?' He chewed his lower lip. 'His nephews? The bastard princes? He must have murdered them, Francis. How can such a King survive?'

I just sat there, refusing to commit myself. I could smell Catesby's fear but, if I let him talk, perhaps he might shed some light on the King's secret matter. Catesby refilled his wine-goblet.

'I know nothing of the Princes,' he murmured, as if talking to himself. 'But have you heard, Francis, of St. Julian the Hospitaller?' I nodded. Who hadn't? William Caxton with his new printing-presses in his shop near the palace of Westminster, had published the legend for all who could read. Despite the warm room, I shivered and caught Catesby's meaningful stare. Julian the Hospitaller was a soldier who had killed his own father and mother, spending years doing penance. God finally appeared to him in a vision to say his sins were forgiven. Had Richard committed such a crime?

'You talk about the future, William,' I said abruptly. 'What do you advise?'

'Nothing dramatic,' he answered. 'If the Tudor lands we stand by Richard. But there are things we can do to show our opponents that our enmity is honourable and not malicious.'

'Such as?'

'The King has hostages, particularly from the Stanley family. They could be our link.' He rose, nervous, as if frightened to talk further. He picked up his cloak, wrapped it around him and once again refused my request to stay the night. We went out into the cold, blustery darkness. A sleepy-eyed groom brought round his horse. Catesby mounted and, gathering the reins in his hands, suddenly leant down towards me.

'Are you with me on this matter, Francis?' I looked back at my darkened house, the faint chink of light from Anne's chamber. I heard the hoot of an owl and the yip-yip of a hunting vixen. I took him by the hand.

'William, tell those who matter, I am with you.'

I did not know if Anne or Belknap had overheard our conversation but, two days after Catesby had left, Anne's father, the Lord Fitzhugh, came on a visit. A tall, weather-beaten man, he always exuded confidence, liking nothing better than feasting, dancing and a good day in the field with his hawks. He adored Anne but our relations had never been cordial. Oh, he had followed Richard like many gentry of the shire but he was more concerned about the price of timber, the enclosure of lands and the wages of labourers than who ruled at Westminster. On that particular day, however, he made every attempt to heal the breach between us. He brought me a kestrel especially imported from the Rhineland, carefully avoiding any talk of politics. He loudly proclaimed that if the Tudor landed he would act as Commissioner of Array and bring out his levies to fight for Richard. Just before he left, we walked, his arms linked through mine and Anne's, away from where his retainers had their horses gathered.

'Francis,' he began. 'If the Tudor comes, you must fight for Richard.' He hugged his daughter closer to stifle any protests. 'He must do it, Anne,' he continued hurriedly. 'The King has sworn an oath, those who are not with him will be counted against him. Both Francis and I will fight for any king crowned with the assent of Parliament.' He turned to face me squarely. 'Is that not so, Francis?'

'Yes,' I replied, 'that is so.' Both Anne and her father grinned broadly, Lord Fitzhugh winking at me as if I was a fellow-conspirator. God, I played the role, but deep in my heart I felt a traitor. I wondered how many more up and down the kingdom, men like Fitzhugh, well served by the King, were now secretly plotting his downfall.

Sure enough, as spring came, royal couriers brought letters to Minster Lovell. They were polite but curt; the King's enemies beyond the seas were still plotting the destruction of the realm. I, Francis, Viscount Lovell, was to act as the King's Commissioner of Array in the southern counties and make all preparations to raise levies and resist any invasion. Once again I bade Anne farewell, only this time she was joyful, a conspiratorial smile on her face as if we both understood a secret pact. Like her father, I was to act loyally, do all I could, but if matters went ill for Richard, I was to ensure my own safety.

First I went to Nottingham, to the castle Richard publicly called his command centre but secretly described as his castle of care for here he had received news about his son's death. He was still anxious, frenetic, but there was some of the old Richard back, the young soldier, eager to see his enemy out in the open and take his chances on the field of battle. He greeted me as if there was no breach between us, embracing, kissing me, even taking a ring from his finger and slipping it onto mine. He clapped me on the shoulder and told me how I had his confidence and once the Tudor was destroyed Norfolk would not be the only peer with a dukedom. But he was sharp enough to sense something wrong. I could not meet his eye. On the few occasions I did, I saw that haunted, hooded look, as if he could smell the treachery on me. The same atmosphere pervaded the council meetings. All were voluble in their praises and recommendations but the camaraderie of previous days was gone. I was relieved to assume my commission and lead my retinue south.

The whispering campaign against Richard had grown louder and spread wider. Men claimed he even wished to marry his niece, Elizabeth of York, and the old accusations about his being an assassin, a usurper, had once again begun to fester. The Stanleys had left court. They protested their loyalty but Richard did not trust them and, as Catesby had inferred, kept Stanley's son, Lord Strange, as a hostage. The summer grew on in

long, hot days as I travelled the southern downs, across
Southampton Water, organising ships, assembling men,
distributing arms, collecting carts and establishing a line
of scurriers to take any news north. I was still torn by
doubts. On the one hand my loyalty to Richard; on the
other, my fears for the future and doubts about the
King's true character. Catesby's suspicions, however,
were soon proved right.

Richard's orders were clear enough, men were to
fight for him on pain of life and limb, to provide arms,
food and men. But I found things difficult. This
gentleman was ill, that gentleman could not leave at the
moment. Barns which were supposedly full were
suddenly empty. Tenants who should have presented
themselves in the village square before my commissioners, secretly absconded. My spies brought in news of
secret covens and conspiracies. Of men assembling late
at night after dark, using the device of the Red Eagle's
claw as a symbol of recognition. I had no illusions about
the cause of this. The Red Eagle was the Stanley device
and that vicious old spider, the Beaufort woman, was
artfully spinning her web. News came from France.
Charles VIII had supplied Henry with men, money and
ships and two mercenary commanders. I forgot the
French one but the other was a captain from the Scots
guards and I shivered: Seigneur Bernard Stewart
D'Aubigny was a fearsome fighter and a devious
general and, with John de Vere, Earl of Oxford, the
Tudor was well served.

July came, the height of summer. Richard sent news
that the Tudor was assembling his men at Rouen, his
ships on the river Seine. He would probably shelter in
Harfleur and make a landing near Southampton. My
commissioners arrayed their men and brought them in,
long dusty lines, men-at-arms and archers. Behind them
trundled wagons piled high with provisions and arms. A
soothsayer claimed the Tudor would land at Poole in

Dorset to march on London. The King's strategy was that whatever the Tudor did, he would be met by two armies – a combined one under Norfolk and myself, while his, Richard's, marched south to reinforce us. The Tudor must have had the devil's own luck, for his small fleet of fifteen ships gave ours the slip and on Sunday, August 7th, landed in Milford Haven in Pembrokeshire. The usurper hoped to raise Wales behind him. He knelt on the sand, kissing the ground, muttering a line from the psalm, 'Judge me, oh God, and discern my cause'. The great Red Dragon banners of Cadwaller were unfurled and Henry marched to the English border. His agents fanned out before him, trying to raise troops, depicting the pathetic Tudor as Arthur come again.

My own scurriers brought in news of the invasion and fresh ones came from Richard. I was to advance north into Bedfordshire, camp near Woburn Abbey and await further orders. The King sent out letters to all his generals and henchmen. Jack of Norfolk soon stirred himself and I watched his troops come in: long lines of tired, dusty men sweating under an August sun, their silver-blue tabards and banners soiled and coated with a thick grey dust. Similar writs were sent to Henry Percy, Duke of Northumberland, and to the Stanleys, but here Richard met with a cool reception. Yes, these men would march but Percy had problems and Stanley claimed he was unwell. Richard immediately imprisoned Stanley's son, Lord Strange. He foiled an escape attempt by this young nobleman and told Stanley he would execute his son at the first sign of treachery. At last two messengers, sweat-soaked and grimed with travel, arrived with the King's orders to join him at Nottingham. They said the King was in good heart, even hunting from his favourite lodge in Sherwood. He believed once his army was mustered he would bring the Tudor to battle and utterly destroy him.

Fifteen

I rode ahead with a small group of retainers to join the King at Nottingham and met him in the castle solar. His mood alternated from black pessimism to prospects of a golden and rosy future. He was nervous, fidgety, refusing to sit down or stand still, pacing the room as he described the situation. He was waiting for Norfolk and Northumberland and other contingents to reach him. Henry Tudor continued to march north, the gates of Shrewsbury and Litchfield being thrown open to greet him. The Stanleys lay between him and Tudor and, Richard grimly confided, he did not know their true intentions. My walk through Nottingham Castle had alerted me to the suspicion and distrust surrounding the King. Catesby avoided me, Ratcliffe was uneasy and nervous. No man knew how the coming battle would fare. The King's buoyancy and show of confidence was false; on the one hand, he was now free of the tension, eager to fight his enemies in the open; but on the other, he knew he did not command the total loyalty of his followers. He chattered away to me as if I had never been absent, ignoring the rumours of how lukewarm my support had grown. In his eyes I had arrived, I would be with him, and that, he pronounced tersely, would be the mark of all men's loyalty once he had secured victory. He asked about Anne, her father, rumours of treachery in the fleet, and what problems I had encountered in arraigning troops. Then he came and stood over me.

'Francis,' he said quietly. 'Is there anything I can do for you? Anything you need?'

'Yes, Richard,' I replied, ignoring his royal titles to secure his attention. 'In three, four days' time we will meet the Tudor's army. We may win and live victoriously or we might die. I ask you this then, as one friend to another: did you kill your nephews?' Richard's face drained of colour. His lips went tight and flames of fury flared in his eyes. He spun on his heel and strode away. I thought he was ignoring me, but he went over to a table, picked up a book and walked back. He turned the pages and I saw the beautiful gold paintings of a Book of Hours. Holding it high in his right hand, his other hand on a gold cross which hung from a chain round his neck, Richard declared:

'Before God, I swear I had no hand in the deaths of my nephews!' He tossed the book into my lap and stalked out of the room.

I listened to his footsteps echo down the stone-vaulted corridor and cursed my own disbelief. Was Richard really innocent? Or was it just another lie? I looked at the Book of Hours: at the back, on the calf-skin cover, in Richard's own handwriting was a long prayer to the Blessed Julian. Time and again the King prayed for release, for peace between himself and his enemies; and appealed to God that, like Susannah in the Bible, he might be freed from false slander and malicious allegations. I got up and placed the book back on the table. I went over to look through one of the arrow-slit windows at the frenetic activity in the courtyard below. The place was full: men-at-arms, neighing horses, carts being loaded, serjeants and knights bellowing orders to the retainers. Was this, I wondered, this coming battle, to be God's answer to Richard? Deliverance from rumour or peace in death?

The following morning, Friday 19th August, the

King led us down from the rock of Nottingham Castle. We took the Southwell road through the wooded aisles of Sherwood Forest across the hills towards Leicester. I despatched a swift note to Anne, ensured my retainers were in good order, and rode alongside Richard, who showed no anger at my question to him the previous day. Behind us, the royal army moved in a square column of march, troops of cavalry on each wing. Richard and the household in the van, our baggage and impedimenta in the centre, and a force of northern lords bringing up the rear. I glimpsed Stanley's son, Lord Strange, amongst them, young, white-faced, fearful lest his father's treachery cost him his head. He was bound hand and foot to his horse.

A little before sunset on the same day, we crossed the river Soar and entered Leicester, up the High Street into the square before All Saints Church. Here, Richard, who had been quiet for most of the march, issued instructions to his camp marshalls, saying he would take up quarters in a nearby inn which bore his badge, the White Boar. The town's cannon roared out a royal salute, messengers bustled their way through, their faces grimy with dust and sweat. They announced the glad news that Norfolk had arrived and Northumberland would be here early the next day. Richard nodded, and whispering he wished to be alone went into the large, cantilevered, half-timbered inn. Behind him, his retainers unpacked his furniture, bed, caskets and other paraphernalia.

The following day, Saturday, 20 August, was frenetically busy. Richard took counsel with his captains and principal commanders about how he should counter the Tudor threat. Earl Henry Percy of Northumberland arrived, his lying face and evasive answers about why he had not come earlier creating a sense of unease, only heightened by the Stanleys' continual refusal to bring their forces over to Richard.

Other levies poured into the town, archers, foot-soldiers, some well-armed, others causing acute dismay to the serjeants and muster captains. One unexpected arrival was Sir Robert Brackenbury with a contingent from London. We met in a narrow street just off the town square. I expected him to either glare or openly ignore me but he just smiled sadly, his eyes dowcast as he stood aside to let my by. I did not speak to Richard. The King would not discuss anything but who was with him, who had not arrived, or the possible intentions of the Stanleys, whilst he uttered grim warnings of what would happen to those traitors after his expected victory over the invaders. Norfolk, eating and drinking as if his life depended upon it, openly boasted how all would go well.

Late that Saturday night, however, when the King had withdrawn, a more grim-faced Norfolk confided to both Catesby and myself how he suspected the King was surrounded by treachery on every side. Catesby stiffened beside me. I had to look away to hide my own embarrassment, but the Duke was lost in his own thoughts. He searched his wallet and brought out a small dirty scrap of vellum which he handed to me. I looked at the spider-thin handwriting, a doggerel verse. I smiled secretly, for Collingbourne would have liked it. The message was stark enough –

'Jack of Norfolk, ride not so bold,
For Dickon, your master, has been both bought and
    sold.'

'I wonder,' Norfolk said, plucking the parchment from my fingers, 'how many such messages have gone out? And what traitors have sold our master?' Catesby and I just sat, not daring to answer.

On Sunday, 21st August, the royal army formed its column of march. The streets of Leicester filled with colour as banners were unfurled to the shrill bray of trumpets. The King, now tight-lipped, his face white, drawn with tension, led the royal army down the Swine's Market, his figure slight, even in the full casing of armour he wore. Richard bore a gold crown upon his helmet; the banners of France, England and St. George snapped and flapped in the breeze above him. All the heralds, in their brilliant tabards, blew shrilly on trumpets, drowning the beat of the drummers, proclaiming that the King was going forth to war to destroy his enemies. Behind Richard was Norfolk and his son, the Earl of Surrey, then other retinues forming a screen around the great baggage-train, and in the rear Northumberland, treacherous as ever. I wished to God the King had killed him on the spot! I was slightly behind the King; unlike him I was not in armour for I wanted to feel the sun and wind and rejoice in that glorious August day. The trees were green still in full bloom, the sky blue, and around us, as far as the eye could see, the yellow corn reaching up ripe and full, ready for the harvest. I thought of Anne and the calm beauty of Minster Lovell. I wished I could turn my horse and canter away from the agony, suspicion and frenetic excitement of the royal army.

Later in the afternoon, the army entered the small village of Sutton Cheyne, a collection of houses grouped along a high street and an old greystone church. The hamlet stood on a ridge, the land sloping northwards to the manor and village of Market Bosworth. Our spies reported that Sir William Stanley had taken up position here and those with keen eyesight could espy the different colours of his banners, pavilions and the liveries of his retainers.

The site was near the old Roman road which the Tudor would have to march along. We camped on the summit of some rising ground the locals called Ambian Hill. This provided us with an excellent view of the low-lying Redmore Plain beneath, whilst our camp was protected by a moss-covered, treacherous marsh. Tents and pavilions were set up, camp fires lit, servants and boys bringing water and provisions from the purveyance wagons. Our spies and scouts went out and returned to declare the Tudor's army was three miles away and nearby the forces of the two Stanley brothers, their intentions still unclear. Darkness fell and the fires of the enemy danced like a cluster of fireflies across the meadow. A restless night, the silence continually broken by the hammering on steel, the clanging of armour, horses neighing and the shouts of camp marshals and sentries.

Richard held a brief council in his tent. We sat grouped round a trestle-table as Norfolk, with the aid of a crudely-drawn map, demonstrated what actions we should follow. Essentially, we would hold the high ground and allow the Tudor to attack, hoping he would waste his energy. However, any real discussion was blighted by distrust of the true intentions of both Northumberland and the Stanley brothers. I looked around the table, for the last time seeing the faces of Richard's secret council, all pale-faced, with black shadows under eyes which gleamed with a frenetic excitement. To be brief, we had no illusions. Tomorrow there would be a battle and it would be a hard-run fight. The Tudor was already proclaiming himself as King and, if we were defeated, we would suffer the fate of any traitor caught in arms against the Crown. The wine-jug circulated. No one wished to leave, preferring to stay in the flickering light of the candles, drawing comfort from those present. At last Richard ordered us to withdraw. Catesby touched me gently on the arm as I left the royal pavilion, a signal to follow him deeper into the darkness. Once out of earshot he turned.

'This is the message,' he whispered. 'Nothing is to be done to Lord Strange, otherwise, if the battle is lost and we are found on the field, it will be either the axe or the rope.' I nodded and turned away, fully understanding Catesby's message. We were not to go over to the Tudor but simply ensure we left the battlefield as discreetly as possible. I walked back to my own tent. I wished Belknap was with me and regretted my decision to send him back to Minster Lovell before marching north to join Richard. I entered my tent, surprised to find the page had lit a candle and placed it on the table. I cursed, such negligence could start a fire and a panic. But then I saw the figure huddled in a cloak seated in the far corner. He stood as I entered, pulling back the cowl, and I recognised the swarthy dark looks of Sir Robert Brackenbury.

'You are welcome, Robert,' I said, realising this was no chance meeting. He had just attended the recent council meeting. He must have left swiftly, to ensure he would be at my tent before I arrived and so block any refusal to see him.

'Sit down, Francis,' he replied, and without another word turned to the two cups standing on a chest, both already filled with wine. He gave one to me. 'Pardon my presumption,' he said quietly, 'but I need the wine and your page was agreeable enough.' I sipped from the cup, watching him carefully. 'I have come to make a confession,' he began abruptly.

'Aren't there priests in the camp?' I asked.

'As a matter of fact, there are not,' he answered. I felt the tingle of excitement in my stomach, the quickening pulse of my heart, and yet smiled at the foolishness of it. Here, before the battle, the evening before I might die, I would learn the truth about a secret which had eluded me for two years. I sat on the corner of the chest close to him.

'Then you had better make your confession, Robert,' I said. 'It is already dark and the King intends to be moving before dawn.'

'I wish to confess,' Backenbury began, 'to the murder of William Slaughter.' He held up a hand to fend off any questions. 'Slaughter was a rogue, a mercenary, corrupted by the traitor Buckingham. When Buckingham came to the Tower,' he hurried on, 'he saw the Princes, as I said, in the royal apartments. I moved them from the Tower to keep them more secure. The chamber you saw was empty. Only Slaughter and I saw the Princes.' Brackenbury rubbed his face. 'Anyway, Buckingham. He gave them gifts, small painted wooden swords and a silver tray of sweetmeats. The dish was poisoned.' He stopped and put his face in his hands. 'The venom must have been some Italian concoction, not quick-acting but slow, taking hours rather than minutes to work.'

'But surely,' I interrupted, 'such presents should have been carefully inspected?'

'Oh, they were.' Brackenbury looked up at me. 'Slaughter told me he would check everything, but he had been bribed. The morning after Buckingham left, the knave came rushing to me, saying how the Princes were sickened, too drowsy even to stand. I ordered him to keep his mouth shut and, by secret passages, brought the Princes to a small chamber deep in the royal apartments, a room once used as a warming-room for any child born in the Tower.' Brackenbury shook his head. Beads of sweat poured down his now grey face. 'There was nothing I could do,' he whispered hoarsely. 'If I sent for Argentine, he would know it was poison. I or the King would be blamed. Richard would never forgive me. I did not want to die a traitor's death.'

'And the Princes?' I asked, hiding the chilling terrors in my own body.

'They just died,' he answered.

'And their bodies?' Brackenbury placed his head in his hands.

'God forgive me. Slaughter and I simply bricked the

room up. We took off the door and lintel, it did not take. long. The chamber lay off a disued passageway, very few people used it. I then wrote to the King saying the Princes had escaped and you know the rest.'

'And Slaughter?' I asked.

'At first,' he replied, 'I swore him to secrecy, offering him gold, treasure, even lands, but afterwards I recollected how the Princes must have died. First I thought it was the sweating sickness but I knew they'd been poisoned and Slaughter had been bribed, so I arranged to meet him in some small squalid tavern alongside Cheapside. I cut his throat.' Brackenbury gulped from his cup. 'He was a traitor and he deserved a traitor's death. I was quick and it was a mercy for him.'

'Surely a new, bricked-up chamber would be noticed?' I said.

'Not really,' Brackenbury said wearily. 'The royal apartments in the Tower are a collection of rambling rooms and chambers. Many are in disrepair. They are hardly ever used.' He looked away, listening to the distant noises from the camp. 'Sometimes in my dreams,' he said, 'I stand in that long, dusty, whitewashed passage looking down at the walled-up chamber.' He licked his lips. 'I hear a tapping, see the dust begin to crumble, a skeletal arm push through the plaster, stretching and grasping for my throat.' In the darkness I heard an owl hoot and, despite the warmth, I shivered.

'But the King?' I asked, asserting myself. 'He must have questioned you?' Brackenbury shook his head.

'No, nothing out of the ordinary. No reproof. No reports. Just a strange look and assurances that he did not hold me responsible. It makes me think.' Brackenbury rose and put his cup back on the table. For the first and last time ever he patted me affectionately on the shoulder. 'Tomorrow, Francis, God be with you. I have confessed my sins.' He walked to the flap of the tent.

'Sir Robert,' I called out. 'You said something then

about the King's manner making you think.' Sir Robert grimaced, rubbing his hand through his hair, and walked back towards me.

'Perhaps it's wishful thinking,' he murmured, 'but, after I became Constable, I never really spoke to the Princes. Remember, I only knew them for ten days and they hardly talked to me. All their old retainers were withdrawn, Argentine included. Slaughter was a stranger.'

'What is it, man?' I interrupted.

'Well,' Brackenbury began slowly, 'I said it was wishful thinking but there were times, when I watched the Princes, I half suspected they were not genuine. Something about them, bearing a close resemblance but not the sons of Edward IV.' He laughed nervously. 'As I have said, the humours of the mind can play strange tricks.' He looked at me. 'Goodnight, Francis.'

I heard him walk away and stood for a few seconds at the mouth of the tent, catching the cool breeze and listening to the sound of the camp settling down for its restless sleep. So the Princes were dead. I thought of that long, whitewashed passage, the sombre dark chamber and its hidden secret. Perhaps Richard knew the truth and blamed himself, fully expecting that tomorrow he would have to settle his debts with God.

Sixteen

Long before dawn our captains moved amongst our sleeping army, rousing soldiers to break their fast and prepare to stand in their battle-lines. I had slept restlessly, fitfully, and woke to the sounds of a stirring camp: the clash of harness, the ringing of armour, the hum of bowstrings, horses neighing and stamping as they were saddled for battle. I hastily drank a cup of watered wine and shouted for my servants to arm me in full harness, breast and back plate, greaves, reinforced gloves, sword, dagger, lance and battle-axe. I went straight to the royal pavilion; Richard also was being armed, the table used for the previous night's council now covered with pieces of the finest armour from Nuremburg. The King looked pale and red-eyed from lack of sleep but confident enough as he stood in the satin-lined fustian doublet, woollen hose with padded kneecaps, and thick leather shoes. His pages were busy dressing him, putting the armoured sollerets on his feet to which gold spurs were attached. Once he was armoured, a loose belt was girded round his waist; on one side hung a triangular-bladed dagger and on the other a naked double-edged sword thrust through an iron ring so it could easily be drawn. Over all, Richard donned a short-sleeved, red and blue silk surcoat, split at the sides, embroidered with the golden leopards and lilies of England and France. Once finished, Richard had a few quiet words with his pages and cradling his helmet, a gold-plated steel sallet surmounted by a golden crown, he walked from his pavilion into the darkness. There, in a dimly-lit ring of spluttering torches, the rest of his captains awaited him. The King, his face grey with anguish and tension, confessed his sleep had been broken by nightmares. One of the captains, I forget whom, hesitatingly reported that there were no priests in the camp to say Mass.

'No need,' Richard snapped back. 'If our quarrel is God's, we need no prayers. And if it is not, such prayers are only idle blasphemy.' Someone else made a pathetic joke about the lack of breakfast. Richard smiled. 'If I gave such orders,' he said, 'spies would have undoubtedly reported to Henry and he would know of our awakening. Let us fight and still have time for breakfast!' The King mounted his tall grey war-horse, his favourite destrier, White Surrey; a squire handed him his principal battle weapons, a lance and battle-hammer. The latter was Richard's chosen weapon, a cruel device; half-axe, half-mallet, it could and would wreak terrible damage in battle. The captains were dismissed, Richard instructing me and others in his household to stand with him in the battle. Our horses were brought and, as we mounted, orders rang out and the army began its ascent of Ambian Hill.

The plan of the previous evening was followed. On the brow of the hill was our van under Norfolk consisting of pikemen, archers and one hundred and forty light serpentines and a number of bombards served by their sooty-faced gunners. Behind Norfolk was Richard with a small hand-picked force of household knights and men-at-arms. In the rear Northumberland, moving sluggishly, ignoring Richard's scurriers who rode up and down insisting the northern earl move quicker. For a brief, quiet moment as our army turned to face down the hill, Richard rode along the ranks shouting encouragement.

'This battle,' he proclaimed, 'will change England for ever! If the Tudor wins there will be destruction and, if I am victorious, I will face no further opposition!' A desultory cheer greeted his words. Richard galloped back to us, the visor of his helmet open, revealing a flushed, excited face, his eyes gleaming at the prospect of battle. He touched me lightly on the cheek and I felt the cold finger of his steel glove before he turned to John Kendall, his secretary.

'John,' he snapped. 'Send out a scurrier, our fastest, to the Lord Stanley. Tell him he either joins our force now or his son loses his head!' Kendall nodded, and turning his horse, galloped away while Richard and the rest stared down the hill where the enemy were beginning to mass. The Tudor army, caught a little by surprise by Richard's speed, were already advancing around the marsh to face us. On our far left the Stanleys still stood in watchful silence. The King glared across, cursing them as traitors. He turned and shouted to those around him:

'Stanley, at least, has not joined Tudor. He waits to read the signs. Let us give him one now!' Orders were rapped out. Above us the royal banners were unfurled to the bray of trumpets and the clash of drawn swords. A scurrier left, riding fast along our ranks towards Norfolk with the King's instruction to advance. The Duke led his ranks a little way down the slope of Ambian Hill. Trumpets rang out and the troops stopped. Norfolk and his marshals arranged their troops in the shape of a bent bow; on its edges were archers, the main host of men-at-arms in the centre. Beneath us the enemy troops advanced rapidly around the swamp, led by the steel-encased figure of John de Vere, Earl of Oxford, easily recognisable under his banner of a soaring star. More orders rang out, trumpets brayed, the armies mocking each other. The King's banner dipped, Norfolk's van stopped. I heard the order to 'Stand' and 'Loose' and a thick cloud of arrows streamed down into Oxford's rank. The killing had begun, the first victims already writhing on the ground. The Tudor had brought some bombards, we heard the crack of guns and stone cannonballs whistled through the air. Our own guns answered, an ear-cracking sound, but they made little impact. The mass of enemy foot-soldiers came on and paused for a while to re-form. Their trumpets shrilled once more, followed by shouted commands in Welsh, French and English, and the rebels began to climb the hill.

I saw Norfolk's blue and silver banner dip once, twice, heard a fresh fanfare of trumpets, and Norfolk led his men down the hill. The two armies collided in a dreadful crash of steel while we above just stood and watched. The two lines swayed backwards and forwards like the ebb of the sea, the sun glinting on battle-axe, sword and spear, plunging silver, rising red. Richard cursed. Our ranks were giving ground. The centre was beginning to bend just where Oxford's golden banner flapped close to Norfolk's. Richard snapped a few commands and a party of horsemen rode down to bolster the line. Norfolk's retreat stopped and Old Jack began his plan to circle the enemy, his troops thinning out to drive the enemy flanks inwards. Oxford's banner dipped once again, his trumpeter shrilling the command to retire to the standards. Swiftly they did so, the enemy massing themselves round the banners of their leaders. Norfolk pulled back a few paces as if puzzled by what was happening. Oxford, using the respite, organised his troops into a thick wedge, the point aimed directly at the hilltop on which we stood. Norfolk's trumpeters sounded the advance and his troops hurled themselves on the enemy. We saw his banner rise then suddenly fall. Richard, alarmed, sent a messenger down to see what was happening. One of his spies came running up to him, talking excitedly; he pointed westwards to a figure on horseback just beneath the Red Dragon standard, surrounded by no more than a dozen men.

'The Tudor!' he shouted excitedly. Richard stood up in the stirrups, visor up, his eyes straining, trying to glimpse his enemy.

Two other messengers rode up, horses lathered in sweat, their faces begrimed with the dust of battle. One brought Stanley's reply: 'Richard could kill Lord Strange for Stanley had other sons'. Richard, his eyes blazing with fury, shouted at Catesby to have the young man's head hacked off. Catesby nodded, but when the King turned away to talk to the other messenger Catesby just looked across at me, his face pale and sweaty under the raised visor, and he shook his head. Richard did not follow the matter up for the second messenger brought terrible news. Norfolk was dead. Old Jack, locked in hand-to-hand combat with Oxford himself, had raised his visor to catch some coolness, only to be caught by an arrow full in the throat. Of his son, Surrey, nothing was known. We looked down the hill. Norfolk's line was beginning to break. Around the banner of the silver lion a savage swirl of fighting men. Ratcliffe shouted, indicating that the King should look back to where Henry Tudor's small party was beginning to move.

'The Welshman!' Ratcliffe shouted. 'He goes to seek Stanley!' Richard smiled thinly, encompassing us all with one dreadful look.

'We shall seek out the Tudor!' he barked. The men of the household began to look to their weapons, helmets were donned, squires running up with lances. Catesby shouted across to the King that he should not go. If things went ill, there was always flight. Richard replied contemptuously:

'Catesby, I intend to live and die a King!' Richard turned full in the saddle, his armour creaking as he looked directly at me.

'Francis, you are with me, as at Middleham? One great charge?' I looked at the King; his face was relaxed, good-natured. I nodded back my answer, lifting my huge lance, the butt against my steel-encased thigh. Other members of the household were also ready. The King closed his visor, lifted his battle-axe and nudged his horse forward at a walk. The household knights paced slowly behind him down the slope, swinging clear of the battle-line. At the bottom of the hill I closed my visor as the King urged his horse into a gallop, faster and faster; all I could see through the eye-slits of my helmet was the King's gold crown. To the left I caught a glimpse of the bright-red jackets of the Stanleys and to my right the still swirling battle-line.

Led by Richard, our force of a hundred mounted men swept down upon the Tudor bodyguard. A huge knight, fully encased in armour, suddenly loomed up before Richard but the King cut him down with one cruel swing of his battle-axe. We followed him through into the Tudor lines, cutting and hacking, steel against steel, axe crashing into flesh and bone, knights reeling out of their saddles, the blood pumping through the slits of their helmets. Richard seemed like a man possessed and I, close behind him, remained unscathed as men either fell or shrank away from the King's dreadful axe. Now we were near the Red Dragon banner. Richard forced his horse forward, slashing and hacking with his axe, sending both banner and bearer down into the dust. I heard fresh shouting to my left: Ratcliffe, leading a fresh horse, pushed by me, shouting at the King, pointing over to our left where the Stanleys had begun to move, their intentions now obvious – they had declared for Tudor. Richard shook Ratcliffe away, still intent on reaching the centre of the Tudor bodyguard and personally killing the invader. But then, like a great river, the Stanley force hit our flanks. They broke up our group as they swirled around that small, dreadful figure in armour who cut and slashed at them with his axe now covered in blood and gore.

I was pushed out of the battle and pulled off my helmet, eager to gasp some air as well as see more clearly what was happening. The force of household knights had ceased to exist. Richard, his helmet now off, was surrounded by a mass of Stanleys. He still fought on as he screamed, 'Treason! Treason!' at the men who had thwarted his last dreadful charge. I saw White Surrey stumble. The King went down. Looking over my shoulder to the right, I saw Norfolk's men had broken, streaming back up to the brow of Ambian Hill. The King was gone. The battle was lost. Other parties of horsemen were now making their presence felt, so I stripped myself of my armour and, turning my mount, galloped like the wind from the battlefield.

I have stopped writing for a while, re-reading my account of the battle outside Sutton Cheney, for my life ended there. I became an outlaw, a wolfshead, one of the living dead who haunt the shadowy twilight places. Yet, I must hasten on. I have food, drink and candles to spare, carefully rationed against the encroaching darkness, but I feel myself getting weaker so I must hurry. I fled like a demon from the battlefield, riding south, my poor horse its great heart pounding as we galloped along secret trackways and paths back into Oxfordshire and Minster Lovell. There was no real pursuit and I outstripped those harbingers of our evil fortune.

Minster Lovell, so beautiful in the August sunshine it wrenched my heart, was deserted. Only Belknap was there. The rest of the servants had either returned to their homes or gone with Anne to rejoin her father, Lord Fitzhugh, until the crisis was over. Belknap heard my account of the battle, his face sombre and passive as he learnt I was no longer Viscount Lovell, Chamberlain to the King, Knight of the Garter, but simply Francis Lovell, an attainted traitor. I knew that the Tudor spies and scouts would be out looking for me so I gave Belknap verbal messages for Anne and hid for days here in my secret chamber. However, I became alarmed at the constant visits to the house of the Tudor's men. One night I slipped secretly away without even leaving instructions for Belknap or messages for Anne.

I hid with various friends and eventually took sanctuary in Colchester Abbey, joining the two Stafford brothers who had also escaped the battle. Those were dark days, shot through with intrigue and mystery. The Tudor sent me messages, offers of pardon, even a role in his coronation at Westminster, but I resolutely refused. The offer was repeated, the bearer being no less a person than the Lord Fitzhugh, Anne's father, but I turned him away. I did not trust the Tudor and, like the Staffords, believed what the usurper had done could be undone. I also felt I had betrayed Richard. He had confided in me, raised me to great heights, yet I had plotted to desert him, believing him to be an assassin; but Brackenbury's confession had ended such doubts. I often thought of Anne, pined for her company and the sight of her sweet face, but I found it impossible to talk to her father. He had been one of those time-servers, like Stanley and Northumberland. I wondered if he had always plotted to desert the House of York. Nor had I forgotten the rancour of many of Tudor's supporters towards me: the Lady Margaret Beaufort had sworn vengeance. I had no intention of being led like a fatted calf to the slaughter.

Belknap came to visit me bearing simple messages from Anne, my retainers and close acquaintances. He also informed me what had happened after the battle. Most of the King's household had been killed with him: Ratcliffe, Kendall, Percy and others. Richard's corpse had been most horribly treated, stabbed and beaten until hardly recognisable before being stripped half-naked, a felon's halter strung around his neck, and slung contemptuously across a horse one of his former heralds had to ride back into Leicester. For two days the body was exposed to public view on the steps of Greyfriars before being tossed into a nameless grave. I wept as Belknap talked, swearing vengeance, knowing deep in my heart that my treatment would be no different if I came out of sanctuary. I used Belknap to pass information to other Yorkists plotting a rebellion around the Easter of 1486; they hoped to raise the north and capture the Tudor as he made his progress through the kingdom.

It was doomed from the start, the Tudor had news of our movements. Perhaps we were frightened. I remembered Collingbourne's famous verse – the Hog was dead, the Rat killed and poor Catesby, the Cat, had been executed after being caught fleeing from the battle. He was hanged, but not before they allowed him the grisly mercy of drawing up his will. Catesby, ever the clever lawyer (as one of my adherents, Sir Thomas Broughton of Lancashire, told me), let it be known that both he and I had had reservations about our former King. In the last clauses of his will, Catesby asked Lord Stanley to pray for his soul and take better care with it than he had his body – a veiled reference to Catesby interceding and saving Lord Strange. Catesby also concluded:

'And if Lord Lovell be admitted to the King's Grace, he to pray for my soul.'

Poor Catesby. He trusted no one, and, unfortunately, no one trusted him.

Our attempted uprising was a failure, betrayed by spies. All I remember are images. Stark, ragged banners black against a lowering sky. Small parties of horsemen galloping from one manor to another, seeking men and support. Ambushes in lonely places, men screaming as the arrows whirred out to gash neck, face and chest. And then, as in Richard's last battle, the feeling of being trapped; lines of steel-cased men searching the meadows, woods and small hamlets for any survivors. The Stafford brothers were taken and I, after one fleeting visit to a now deserted Minster Lovell to draw monies from my secret chamber, fled abroad to Tournai in Hainault. There, the Dowager Duchess Margaret, sister to Richard III, gave me and others shelter, fuelling our hatred for the Tudor, promising us men and supplies.

Seventeen

Tournai was welcoming enough but Margaret's court was full of shadows and ghosts. Our quarters were comfortable, even luxurious. However, I fretted like some stabled horse, finding it difficult to shake off the spectres of the past. I received a letter from Anne; it was cold and distant; rumours of plots by other supporters of the House of York but they were nothing. Vapid smoke, no real fire, and always tinged with danger for we never knew if the Tudor and his legion of spies were behind them. Oh, the Tudor was a clever one. He grasped the crown tighter than Richard ever had, using Bishop Morton and his mother's chaplain, Christopher Urswicke, to ferret out secrets, unearth plots and destroy any opposition of him.

All I could do was dally around the taverns and meeting-houses of Tournai, remembering the past and wondering what to do next. Time and again I went over the King's secret matter, my suspicions being aroused by news from London. Strange, the Tudor had made no accusations against Richard, no startling revelations, no proof, no evidence. What, I wondered, had happened to that grisly, secret chamber in the Tower? The Tudor wanted to marry Elizabeth of York, even honouring the Woodville woman. Surely, they must have some influence and insist that a future husband or prospective son-in-law should reveal the truth about the two murdered Princes? Nothing. Ominous silence.

Veiled hints. All shadows, no substance.

I thought I would end my days as a pensioner of the Dowager Duchess, when fortune gave her wheel another fickle turn. Other exiles came to Tournai, including John de la Pole, Earl of Lincoln, Richard's nephew, who had made his peace with the Tudor but now regretted it and fled abroad seeking vengeance. A popinjay of a man, vain, stupid, I never really trusted him. The Dowager greeted him like a long-lost son. I was polite but cool, though my heart warmed to see Sir Edward Brampton in his retinue. Still dressed as gaudily as a peacock, Brampton had returned to his privateering in the Channel after the Tudor's victory. We exchanged greetings and Brampton whispered that he wished a secret meeting as soon as possible, mentioning the name of a small tavern just off the market square in Tournai. I met him there shortly after dark, a gloomy, low-beamed place with rushes on the floor and few pretensions to luxury though I could see why Brampton had chosen it; full of nooks and corners, it was the ideal place for conspirators to meet. Sir Edward was already there, tense with excitement, his eyes and pure white teeth flashing in the darkness, the bells sewn on his jerkin clinking at every movement. He hired a small table, shouting for the best wine the house had and damning the inn-keeper to mind his own business and keep well away.

Brampton leaned across the table and held my wrists tightly.

'Do you remember the King's secret matter, Francis? The fate of the Princes?' I nodded guardedly. Brampton's face was flushed with excitement and he licked his lips as if savouring a good wine.

'Well,' he added, 'I believe one of the Princes is still alive. I have seen him.' I would have pulled away but for the vice-like grip on my wrists.

'That is ridiculous!' I said. Brampton gazed at me steadily. 'Where?' I exclaimed. 'When?'

'You were in the same camp as he, the night before the fatal battle.'

'Sir Edward,' I said quietly. 'Tell me and have done with it.'

Brampton took his hands away, steepling his fingers.

'Do you remember that last council meeting? Well, after Richard dismissed us and all his attendants, saying he wished to be alone, I followed the rest out. A few hours later, unable to sleep because of the impending battle and knowing the King was in a melancholy mood, I went back to the royal tent. I thought the King was alone until I saw his secretary, Kendall, bring a boy into the royal tent. He must have been nine or ten years old. There was something about him vaguely familiar, the way he walked, held his head. I kept in the shadows and went along the side of the pavilion. In their haste the servants had not erected it properly and there were gaps between the overlapping sheets. I found one which gave me a view of what was going on. Kendall had gone, God knows where, and Richard was alone except for the small boy, thin, pale-faced. Richard was holding him gently by the arms. The King murmured something about not recognising him and that he would have to leave for if the coming battle went badly and the King's enemies knew the boy was alive, they would undoubtedly murder him. Richard pulled the boy to him, embraced him passionately, kissing him on either cheek. The King called out and Kendall returned.' Brampton stopped speaking and poured the now empty wine-cups to the brim, offering one to me. 'You remember the confusion the following morning? Kendall looked tired, travel-weary. I asked him where he had been. His answer was diffident. I pretended to be suspicious for we all knew there were common rumours about traitors in the camp. Kendall explained he had been to Eastwell, I think it was there, on a private mission.' Brampton shrugged. 'Then he just walked away. That's all I know.'

I leaned back on the bench and stared up at the rafters. Brampton was telling the truth, but about what? Richard's words about recognising the boy indicated that the lad may have been an illegitimate son. If so, why had Richard not mentioned him? He had made no attempt to hide his two other illegitimate children, John and Katherine. Indeed, he had boasted about them, taking every care to lavish honours, dignities and lands upon them. And why should the King be concerned that the Tudor, if victorious, would persecute and harass a young illegitimate son? Why didn't the King afford similar protection to his two bastard children or the son of his brother, the Earl of Warwick? Why the secrecy? Why was it so important to send Kendall through the night to hide the boy away?

'Do you realise, Francis, what this means?' Brampton interrupted excitedly. 'Richard was no assassin. Perhaps the boy *was* one of the Princes, so a direct claimant to the House of York still lives in England.' I put my hand over his.

'Edward, let us tread gently here. Does Lincoln know this?'

Brampton shook his head. 'No, I do not like the man and I tell you this, Francis, I am going back to privateering, perhaps returning to Portugal. Lincoln has the stink of defeat and treachery around him.'

'Good,' I replied. 'Let us leave it at that.' Brampton left shortly afterwards, slipping into the night, leaving me to my thoughts. Two things convinced me Brampton was not relaying rumour. First, his story made sense. Richard had been mysterious about the two Princes, almost apologetic to me, as if frightened to let me into a secret. His meeting with the young boy just before the battle accorded with his mood. Richard had been anxious, withdrawn, fearful of what was to come. Secondly, Brackenbury also had his suspicions and so the two confessions interlinked, forming a pattern.

Perhaps there was hope, but Brampton's story created more problems than it solved. Was this boy one of the Princes? If so, where was the other and who was buried in that secret chamber in the Tower?

During the next three days I attended countless meetings with Lincoln and the Dowager Duchess. Lincoln unfolded his plans, claiming we had lost against the Tudor for two reasons. First, he had been assisted by professional mercenaries. Secondly, Richard's reputation had been tarnished, albeit falsely, by rumour and slander. If we invaded England, we would need mercenaries of our own. Lincoln turned and bowed towards the Duchess, the Princess Margaret had promised these, two thousand German lancers under their captain, Martin Swartz. Finally, we would need a figurehead and Lincoln described the most sensational of plots. How an Oxford priest, Richard Symonds, held a boy, Lambert Simnel, with the same blond hair and aristocratic looks of the House of York.

'We will,' he claimed triumphantly, 'depict this boy as the young Prince Richard, son of Edward IV, and so draw support from all the country!' I looked around the room, my heart sinking at the insanity of such a plan. Tudor, at least, had been a figure in exile, a Lancastrian prince. But would people rally behind a mysterious boy claiming to be someone the country had now forgotten? The Dowager Duchess was enthused with excitement, eyes gleaming, her sallow face flushed with fervour. She was a woman who would support anyone, be it a monkey or an ape from Barbary, if it suited her plans. Lincoln was lost in his own arrogance. Brampton's eyes simply slid away as if he already knew the outcome of such a madcap scheme. The rest, however, petty Yorkshire gentry, exiles from England, slumped back in their chairs crowing with excitement. I had only one fear. If Simnel used the name Richard of York and was victorious, the young Prince hidden away would still be threatened.

'My Lord,' I interrupted. 'Would not such a scheme founder?'

'Why?' Lincoln's narrow face became creased with annoyance, lips pursed, eyebrows raised like some parish schoolteacher, angry with a favourite pupil.

'Because, my Lord,' I answered wearily, 'God forgive me, but the two Princes must be dead, or lost to us now. Why not have Simnel represent the living and at the same time cast bloody doubts on the Tudor as *he* did on the late King Richard? Who knows,' I jibed, 'if Edward, Earl of Warwick, Clarence's son, has been left alive in the Tower? The Tudor may well have executed him.' I saw the Dowager Margaret's head nodding vigorously. Brampton smiling secretively, also murmured fervent support for my scheme.

After heated debate and constant flattery on my part, Lincoln changed his mind and accepted my plan.

Brampton left shortly afterwards and his words were prophetic. Even now, I find it hard to describe the bloody fiasco. At the end of April we sailed from Tournai and joined Simnel in Ireland on the 5th May proclaiming the silly lie that he was Edward of Warwick. My only comfort was that undoubtable soldier of fortune, Martin Swartz. With his cropped hair, weather-beaten brown leathery skin and pale blue eyes, Swartz instilled confidence and determination into the small group of Yorkist exiles and his two thousand steel-harnessed German mercenaries. A brave man, a good soldier. The Dowager Duchess Margaret must carry his blood on her hands. He deserved a better fate. In Dublin the Irish lords greeted us fervently. They dazzled our eyes with their shabby opulence, lavish banquets and promises of thousands of wild kerns, the Irish foot-soldiers, badly armed, poorly led but with all the bravery of bull mastiffs. Symonds I disliked as soon as I met him, a shabby, sly-faced priest, but I was impressed with Simnel. A good actor, the boy would have made a fortune with any travelling troupe. Nevertheless, I hid my doubts, attending his coronation as King Edward VI in Dublin Cathedral with my fellow-conspirators. Lacking a crown, we took a silver chaplet from the statue of the Virgin and placed it on the pretender's young blond head.

On 4th June we landed at Furness in Lancashire but not with as many Irish kerns as I would have liked. But at least, the red-haired, russet-bearded Irish leader, Thomas Geraldine, came to die with them. We decided to strike east, keeping the north behind us, hoping the levies would come in. A few did but not enough to ensure a victory. Twelve days later, John de Vere, Earl of Oxford, put an end to our fantasies near the small village of Stoke in Nottinghamshire. The battle, despite success at the beginning, was a disaster. Swartz's mercenaries stood and fought to the last man while the Irish were trapped in a narrow gully leading down to the river Trent and slaughtered in their thousands. We had hoped to smash de Vere's forces before fresh royal troops arrived but we were unable to. In one final dramatic charge, which reminded me bitterly of King Richard's death, Swartz, Lincoln and other leaders were trapped and killed. Their bodies were later impaled for public view.

God knows I would have died with them. I fought that day like a berserker, trying to break through Oxford's ring of steel. I wanted to drive my axe into the body of the man who had cost Richard the throne and myself everything I held dear, but I was driven back. I had one final task to accomplish, so I turned my horse down the riverbank and across the Trent to safety. Discarding my armour, I rode across the shire border into Leicestershire, along isolated narrow lanes, my horse's hooves pounding like the beat of a drum. Now and again I would stop, look round, and, satisfied there was no pursuit, hasten on. The night before the battle at

Stoke I had studied Lincoln's crudely-drawn map and, from my own experience, I knew which country tracks and bridle-paths to follow. At times they narrowed to little more than alleyways between the trees. The overhead branches blocked out the sun, making the tracks as dark as any street in Southwark. On one occasion, I met a shepherd guiding his flock to pasture. I scattered them all, ignoring the fellow's shouts as I rode my horse through.

At last I breasted a hill and there in its cusp was Eastwell, a scattering of houses nestling round an ancient single-spired church and, at the far end, I glimpsed a makeshift market and the striped awnings of its booths and stalls. I went into the town, my mud-stained, blood-scarred horse and unkempt appearance drawing hostile mutters and glances. A mongrel came up, lip curled, yellow teeth bared, but I turned my horse which lashed out one iron-shod hoof and the mongrel slunk away. Women hurried out of the houses, drawing back the leather covers which served as doors. They shooed aside the bony chickens pecking in the dust and drew the grimy, naked children closer to their tattered skirts. I hobbled my horse outside the church and, running up the steps, pounded with the hilt of my dagger on its great iron-studded door. The priest came, huffing and puffing, his bald head tinged with a fine sheen of sweat, wiping mud-stained hands on a black, tattered robe. He studied me curiously, the light-blue eyes in his sunburnt face cool and watchful.

'What is it, my son?' The voice was soft, twanging with the local dialect. I pushed by him into the coolness of the church, unsheathed my dagger and slumped exhausted at the base of one of the pillars.

'Father,' I replied. 'I mean no harm, I swear.' I waved my hand towards the darkened altar. 'I swear by the sacraments! By the Bible! By any relic you wish to bring! I mean no harm to anyone in your village but I look for

a boy, blond-haired, about twelve years of age, a
stranger here.' The priest came and crouched beside
me, his eyes studying me carefully. 'Father,' I pleaded, 'I
must see this boy! I must talk to him! Surely, in a village
this size you know everyone.' The priest continued to
gaze at me. 'Father,' I said, 'I mean no harm to the boy
but, soon, I am going to die. I ask you for the love of
Christ, let me see him, let me talk to him. Here, in this
church!' The priest cocked his head sideways, his face
turned away as if listening for something. 'What is it,
Father?' I asked anxiously.

'Nothing,' he murmured. 'Just the master mason and
his apprentice. They are at work on the outside of the
church.' He turned and smiled at me. 'It's the wind, you
see. It howls right down, drenching the brickwork with
rainwater.'

'Father,' I answered wearily, 'please help me.'

'Oh, I will,' the priest replied. 'You see, the apprentice
is not from these parts. A well-spoken boy. He has been
here two years. He and the mason journey from
Leicester to work. Fine craftsmen.' I stirred to get up
but the priest crouched beside me. He suddenly drew
his hands from beneath his robes and laid the tip of a
long, wicked dagger he had concealed there against my
chest. 'Do not move,' he said quietly. 'and even if you do,
you can't see Watkins over there, can you?' I turned,
peering down the dark nave, and saw a shadow move
near one of the far pillars. 'Watkins,' the priest
continued drily, 'is a farmer. He was talking to me when
you began your pounding on the door. I must add that
he is also a fine archer. By now he has a goose-tipped
arrow notched to that wicked longbow of his. He has a
good eye. I am sure he could take you.' The priest
pricked the dagger into the softness of my neck. 'Right
here!' The priest beamed. 'Oh, we have seen the armies,
the great men of war. And you must be one of them. Or
rather were, for now you are fleeing for your life, ay?'

He pulled the dagger away from my neck. 'There must be a reward for you.' I felt slowly for my own purse and emptied its contents, gold and silver Flemish coins, into my hands.

'Take these, Father,' I said. The priest smiled.

'I will take half. You can see the boy, but Watkins and I will stay over in the shadows there. If you threaten the lad, Watkins will put an arrow straight into your heart. I would then take the rest of your coins and turn your corpse over to,' he screwed his eyes up as if puzzled, 'to the Tudor's men,' he said. 'Yes, your arrival here must mean the Tudor has won. May heaven,' he turned and spat, 'may heaven damn him!' He got up and went back to the door. A few minutes later he returned, a tall, blond-haired boy behind him. The lad was dressed in brown woollen leggings, a white soiled shirt and a sweat-stained leather jacket across his shoulders. I looked at the blond hair, the thin narrow face and wide-spaced blue eyes. I knew this must be no other than Richard, Duke of York, son of Edward IV, nephew of Richard III, the last real Yorkist claimant to the crown of England. I struggled to my knees and bowed; the priest gave a sharp intake of breath. 'I don't know who this is, Richard,' he murmured, 'but he seems a good, though now lost, man. He wishes to speak to you. I think he should.' The priest looked at me sharply. 'Though only the sweet Christ knows why.' And, nodding to the apprentice, the priest walked away as the boy knelt opposite me, sitting back on his heels, his hands resting in his lap.

'What is it, sir?' The boy's voice was soft, though already I could catch a rustic burr. I looked in his eyes, used to laughter I think, but now they were guarded and wary. I gazed around; the priest was now over in the shadows.

'Sire,' I answered hastily, 'I am a doomed man. My executioners may well be close behind me, but you must know that I, Francis, Viscount Lovell of Titchmarsh, served your father, King Edward, and your uncle, King Richard. Many times I have fought for your House, but the White Rose has died and soon I will join it.' The boy never moved. He just sat, studying my eyes as if undecided whether to speak or not. 'I mean no harm,' I said. 'I have not come to hurt you but to ask for the love of the sweet Christ what has happened to you, to your brother?' I saw the eyes blink to hide the pain. I shook my head, forcing back the tears of desperation. 'I may have done you and yours great harm.' I knelt before him. 'But now a dying man, I beg forgiveness and ask only for the truth.' The boy leaned over and gently touched my cheek, before crouching cross-legged in front of me.

'I remember you, Viscount Lovell, faintly. I saw you once at Court. You made my father laugh, some joke on a long-forgotten sunny day. Really, I should hate you, for you supported my uncle's usurpation, but I should thank you too, for where is King Richard now? Just a soiled corpse in some ditch! And you, one of his principal generals, crouched in the dust, begging my forgiveness. Yet, where should I go? Back to my mother who handed me over?' I looked up and stared curiously at this boy with the angelic face of a twelve-year-old and eyes a thousand years old, hardened by the experiences he had suffered.

'I will tell you the truth,' he replied quickly. 'My brother and I were placed in the Tower. I remember it was the height of summer. Edward was sick, feverish, never very strong. He became melancholic when he heard of Richard's usurpation, the flight of my mother, the Queen, and the death of Earl Rivers and others. He wanted to die. He caught a fever, some ague from the river.'

'When was this?' I asked.

'At the beginning of June.'

'Before Brackenbury became Constable?' The boy looked puzzled.

'Who was he?'

I almost laughed. Of course, poor Brackenbury. Who was he? The young prince had never seen him. I knew what he was going to say next.

'Uncle Richard,' the boy continued, 'came to see us in the Tower. He became alarmed at Edward's condition and one night secretly moved us.'

'By himself?'

'Yes, alone. Oh, there were guards. They were on the river in boats. All I can remember are their shadows and torches lashed to prow and stern. About three in number. Richard gave me a cloak and a hood to wear. He carried Edward by himself.' The boy looked sharply at me. 'Of course, there were the others.'

'Who?'

'Two boys, of similar height to ourselves. They came into the room in the White Tower. Richard himself made them strip and wear clothes, ours which he had pulled from a trunk. The King told them it was a game, a trick, a device. They were schooled well, not to talk much, not to be afraid as all our servants had been withdrawn. then we left. We landed at some steps where a small carriage awaited us, more soldiers on horseback; the city streets were empty, quiet. Edward was groaning for he was racked with fever, soaking in sweat. We came to a great house. I was placed in one chamber, Edward in another. I never saw my brother again. I think he must have died in the night.' He stopped, biting his lip in an attempt to keep calm. 'I was moved to a merchant's house,' he continued, 'a kindly old man, once a master mason. My uncle took me there, whispering that I was not to tell anyone who I was but pose as his illegitimate issue. I was frightened, scared, yet happy to be free of the Tower. Richard said if I told anyone the truth, I would have to go back to the Tower.' The youth smiled half-heartedly. 'Believe me, Viscount Lovell, it was not hard to keep silent. The merchant was kindly and three days later we left, crossing the river. The merchant told me about his trade, showing me around one of the royal palaces where his own masons were working. He allowed me to join in; it was the first time since my father died that I was happy. Sometimes I thought about my father. My mother ...' He stopped and shook his head. 'I could not think of her. All I knew was that I was happy, pleased to be free of the Tower. I had been so frightened of the guards and the strange powerful men who came to look at me there.' He stopped, licking his lips nervously. 'Then the Tudor landed. My uncle Richard sent messages. I was to be brought north, quickly and quietly, by the King's secretary though he did not know who I was. He brought me into the King's camp. My uncle spoke to me. He said if the battle went well, he would look after me, but if the day went wrong I was to remain hidden. I must not tell anyone the truth, not even that I was bastard issue, for they would not only send me back to the Tower but undoubtedly kill me. The King's secretary took me to Leicester. We were to come here, to Eastwell, but he was so frightened of the Tudor's spies and horsemen, he left me just inside the city gates with some silver and a letter from the master mason in London. I was to stay near the church of Greyfriars until someone came to collect me. The monks looked after me. I saw my uncle's body being brought back.' He closed his eyes. 'It was dreadful! Naked! Splattered from head to toe with red mud. He had been tied like a pig and slung across a horse. The brothers would not let me near him and the next evening a mason came. He is outside now, a kind, cheerful man. Sometimes when I work alongside him, if I close my eyes and listen to his laughter, I think he is my father come back again to jest and tease me.' He stopped and stood up, wiping off the dust of the church floor with his hands. 'Your cause,' he began quietly, raising a hand to fend off any questions, 'the cause of my father, my uncle, my brother, it is finished! You are finished, my Lord! And so am I with any trappings of the Court. For what shall I do? Reveal myself? Join my cousin Warwick in the Tower? No! Sudden death seems the fate of Princes. I am happy and safe as a stonemason. Goodbye! We shall not meet again!'

'Sire,' I said wearily, struggling to one knee. I held my hand out. 'Please.' He came back, slipping his long, sunburned fingers into mine. I kissed them fiercely, holding his cool hand against my flushed cheek. Finally, he pulled it gently away and walked out of the darkness into the early evening sunlight.

I left Eastwell and, by secret routes, rode furiously back to Minster Lovell. Perhaps I could see Anne, just once, take silver from my secret chamber and journey abroad, first to Flanders and perhaps join Sir Edward Brampton, and then go on to Portugal. I had done my duty, fought the good fight. I had kept faith. There was nothing more to do. I had lost everything. I was tired of power, of the malice, the intrigue, the battles and constant bloodshed. Richard would surely understand. Never once had I betrayed him or the secret matter.

Postscript

I approached Minster Lovell secretively, leaving the road and riding across country into the shadow of the trees. The manor house looked deserted. I left my horse in the wood and stealthily approached a small postern door at the back of the house. The windows were all shuttered, no sign of life; the stables were empty, closed and locked. I tapped gently on the door, still no sound; growing bolder I pounded with the pommel of my dagger until I heard faint footsteps. The door swung open and Belknap emerged, an old robe of mine thrown across his shoulders. He was welcoming enough, though, on reflection, he was also secretive, sly, as if he expected my return. In a few short words I described the defeat at East Stoke, Belknap shaking his head when I asked him about Anne. I felt exhausted and, for the first time ever, showed Belknap my secret chamber. Again, he did not seem too surprised, saying he would bring more candles, wine and food. I am glad I did not let him into the room and confide in him further or show him the small secret closet in which I kept monies and most of my private papers. He brought a platter of cold meats, pouring me a full glass of wine, solicitously saying I should take my rest on the trestle-bed for he would wake me in a few hours. Perhaps I should have sensed the danger; Belknap was a good steward but never a body-servant.

Oh, I was wakened all right, by Belknap shaking me

roughly. I sat up in bed, surprised to see my servant now armed with sword and dagger, an arbalest in his hand, the bolt already placed. Behind him, seated at a table, smiling benignly at me from beneath his hood, was John Morton, Bishop of Ely, the Tudor's most zealous counsellor. My own dagger and sword had gone and, while I had been asleep, Belknap or some other had placed an iron chain and gyve around my ankles, the end of it being tethered to a hook on the wall. Morton grinned.

'Ah, well, Master Lovell,' he quipped. 'You have slept well. Almost a full day. We have been looking after you. Your erstwhile comrades are dead, strung up on gibbets outside East Stoke. We missed you and I thought you might come here. Belknap informed us you had a secret chamber.' The Bishop stopped and looked around. 'But nothing so well devised and cunningly hid as this. We might have taken you before. Ah, yes ...' He must have seen the stupefaction on my face and, rising, waddled across to Belknap, clapping a hand on his shoulder. 'Ah, yes, you failed to realise. Thomas Belknap, your erstwhile steward, is also one of my best spies.' The Bishop's white, podgy face beamed at my servant before turning to stare at me. His eyes were like two small black puddles of ice. No warmth, no compassion, only hatred stoked by years of exile.

'Belknap,' he continued smoothly, 'told us everything. Of the King's secret matter, of your running round in the dark. Of your plans to seize King Henry in Brittany. Thomas was always there.' He smiled thinly. 'I shall always be grateful for his services in offering to lead Sir Richard Ratcliffe to me after the late Duke of Buckingham's abortive rebellion.' He put an arm round Belknap's shoulder, pulling him closer as if he was a favourite dog. 'I shall never forget the dance he led them.' The Bishop cocked his head to one side as if uncertain of how to deal with me. I just sat and glared at both of them. Belknap, God forgive him, could not meet my eyes, whilst the fury seething in Morton's eyes warned me not to beg for any mercy from this most implacable of enemies.

'The King's secret matter,' I said. 'The fate of the Princes. You know about them?' I smiled. 'Was it your idea?' Morton nodded.

'Oh, yes. Buckingham was with us from the start. Remember, he had me transferred into his custody? At my bidding, he advised that the Princes be put in the Tower, counselling the stupid Richard to go on a royal progress of the kingdom.' The Bishop sat down, folding his hands together as if in prayer, fully relishing the situation. 'It was easy to turn Buckingham's mind, to stoke his jealousy and hatred. We simply asked him for some symbol of friendship, for some sign of recognition, something which would win the heart of Henry Tudor.'

'The murder of the Princes?' I interjected. 'You had them killed? But you said "we" not just you. That bitch of a Beaufort woman, she was involved as well?' I saw the flicker of alarm in the Bishop's eyes and knew I had hit the mark.

'What other crimes?' I jibed. 'The Princes' father, King Edward IV, was that your work? Were you planning it from the start?' The Bishop shrugged.

'It is all God's will, but sometimes we have to help.' His voice grew shrill. 'The House of York had no right to rule, never had. We are God's agents on earth, the rightful King now sits on the throne at Westminster.'

I felt tired, dispirited. This man, allied with the Beaufort woman, had fought the House of York for twenty-five years and had finally brought it crashing to the ground. Of course, it all made sense. Edward IV suddenly taken ill; some suspicion thrown on Richard; Buckingham playing on Richard's fears; the removal of the Princes, their incarceration in the Tower and a brilliant whispering campaign against Richard which never really ended. I glared across at Morton but found it hard to turn and stare at Belknap standing quietly beside him. A traitor from the start, planted like a weed in my own household, sowing dissension and suspicion. I remembered the attack on me outside the Tower when he had so opportunely appeared and knew it was all his work. A black rage stirred inside me. I could have howled like a trapped wolf but I thought of Eastwell Church and the young face of the hidden Prince Richard. First I smiled and then began to laugh. I put my face in my hands, my shoulders shaking with merriment at this most private of jokes. Morton banged the table with his fist. When I looked up his face had lost its aura of superiority, of vindictiveness.

'You find this amusing?'

'Yes,' I replied. 'I find you amusing. Your secret plans. Your stratagems. Your belief that you control everything.' I raised my right hand. 'I swear,' I said, 'I swear as I now undoubtedly face death; I swear on the sacraments; that Buckingham did not kill the Princes in the Tower. He thought he did but they escaped. One still lives. Do you understand me, Morton? Go, tell that to the Beaufort woman and to her Welsh misbegotten usurper of a son! The House of York still lives!' I placed my wrists together. 'Come,' I said. 'Bind my hands. Gag me. Take me to London or execute me secretly, it won't change the truth.'

Morton rose, no mockery now, his face serious. He came and stood over me.

'You say a Yorkist prince still lives?'

'I do.'

'You swear that?'

'I do and will again.' Morton stepped back a pace.

'Then this is my judgment, Viscount Lovell. You will not be taken from here.' His eyes swept round the room. 'There is some food here, some wine, candles.'

He nodded back towards the table. 'Even writing-materials. You will stay here immured in this chamber. Should you wish to be released, I am sure Belknap will hear your cries and we will release you on condition you tell me where this Prince is. Your estates are forfeit to the Crown. No one will be allowed in.' I rose and edged closer to the Bishop, walking to the end of my chain, not caring when Belknap clicked the crossbow back.

'I tell you this, Bishop. Satan will enter heaven first, before I ever talk to you again. Now take your ...' I gestured towards Belknap, 'your dog, your mongrel, and do your worst!' Morton shrugged.

'So be it!' he replied. Belknap released the chain from the wall and followed his bishop out. He kept his face constantly towards me, the crossbow raised, but I turned my back, preferring to look at the blank chamber wall. They sealed my chamber. I heard Belknap place the bricks. He must have covered them with plaster, perhaps hiding his handiwork behind some arras or tapestry. The door had always been well concealed, it would not take much work to hide it completely. No one would be allowed near the house. I know I will be dead before any of my servants ever return.

I have sat here in the darkness; the vents and cracks allow a little air but I have not been able to tell day from night; I just sit and write in the flickering light of guttering candles. I will ask for mercy. I have written the truth. I have begged God's forgiveness and tried to forgive those who have brought me so low. I have written my confession, my story. Sometimes as the food is scarce, I sit here at this table fitfully sleeping, or remembering the past. I served a king, not a saint, but a prince of his own dark days, who did what he thought best.

I now see the picture complete, the shadows removed by the torch of truth: Richard took the throne from his nephews only to find them sickening in the Tower. I know Richard, he would have panicked. If the boys died, he would be their murderer. He may have even suspected poison, hence their removal at the dead of night. Perhaps Richard meant to return them there, take them north to Sheriff Hutton or even send them to Margaret in Burgundy. Young Edward's death thwarted this. In a quandary, Richard realised the two imposters in the Tower also posed a threat, though not immediately. All the Princes' servants had been withdrawn and replaced by two relative strangers, Brackenbury and William Slaughter. God knows who these unfortunate boys were, but Edward IV and George of Clarence sired enough bastards to people a small village. Richard did not tell Buckingham but kept the secret to himself. Instead he plotted further: the two imposters were to be spirited out of the Tower by Buckingham who could never allege Richard was guilty of their murder. True, Buckingham might have seen through the sham but would he really know? First, Richard could always silence any doubts. Secondly, Buckingham had scarcely met the Princes: during Edward IV's reign he was most conspicuous in his absence from Court. Any changes in the boys' looks or behaviour would be explained by their imprisonment and fall from power. If Lambert Simnel could be recognised by Margaret of Burgundy as her nephew, Buckingham would accept two imposters as princes.

I thought about this carefully, for here Richard made another mistake: Buckingham didn't really care for Richard, the Princes or, above all, anything to do with the Woodville clan. All Buckingham knew was that when he left the Tower, the two boys would soon be dead and the guilt laid at Richard's door.

Richard, however, thought his plan had gone ahead: Brampton would never have really known whether they were Princes or not, whilst Margaret of Burgundy, married and out of England some seventeen years ago, would hardly recognise the boys. She, too, hated the Woodvilles, preferring to see her own brother on the throne than give Elizabeth Woodville the title of Queen Mother. Richard's tortuous mind had worked out this complex plot but he did not know other players had entered the game. Buckingham was being controlled by Beaufort and her minions.

Brackenbury, too, played his role. A man who could be totally trusted, a member of Richard's household, a northerner, someone who did not really know the Princes. In a sense Richard's trust in him was betrayed. Brackenbury, fearful of what Buckingham had done and wishing to protect both himself and the King, simply disposed of the bodies and, until the night before he died, stoutly maintained that the Princes had simply vanished. Richard had no choice but to accept this for he recognised his own guilt in the story. Desperately Richard tried to attempt a solution. He used me, one of his closest friends, to establish the truth. Already guilty at the death of young Edward, the King also had on his conscience the possible death or disappearance of the other two boys. In the end he came full circle. Because of the boys' disappearance, he had to face the nightmare, the dreadful accusation, of having slain two of his own kin. Richard was trapped. Whichever way he moved, who would believe him? Poor troubled Richard! As I approach death, I wonder if he too looked for its peace in that last dreadful charge against the Tudor?

Sometimes I am back with Richard, playing in the reedy marshes outside Middleham Castle or walking with him along a corridor, arms linked, discussing some matter of state. Then there is Anne and I long for her sweet face and teasing ways. One day she will realise how Belknap poisoned her mind against me. I have given my last will and testament. Even if they break in they will not find these papers in their secret compartment.

I know death has taken up position, crouched at my elbow. He waits for me to die but I am not afraid. After the heat of the day, its troubles and strife, perhaps it's best to yield gracefully to the silence of the coming night. I rose high in life, tasted the bitter-sweet fruits of success, but I was no traitor. I kept faith to my King and to that Prince who sat so humbly opposite me in Eastwell Church. If my death buys his life, the price has not been too high in deciding the fate of a Prince.

Author's Note

RICHARD III

The person of Richard III as depicted in this, Lovell's chronicle, seems fairly accurate. Richard was no saint. He was a 15th century warlord who fought for political survival. Like his contemporaries, indeed, like many politicians, he was constantly confronted by a range of choices. He had been loyal to Edward IV but he had no illusions about the Woodvilles and considered the deposition of the two young boys was warranted. The removal of his nephew, the arrest of Hastings and others, as well as the brutal crushing of Buckingham's rebellion are generally true. The same is true of his love for the city of York, his attempts to recapture the Tudor and his deep distrust of both the Stanleys and the Lord Northumberland, his relationship with his mother and his sister Margaret. Nevertheless, although he destroyed all opposition, he did so quite publicly and was totally loyal to those faithful to him. His mental agitation, the endowment of chanceries, the anguished prayer to St. Julian the Hospitaller, are all based on fact. The same is true of his mental state before the battle of Bosworth though even his enemies bore witness to his fighting courage and brave death. At the same time Richard was the object of a sustained propaganda campaign which would have been the envy of any modern secret service and this did not stop with his death. The brutal treatment of his corpse was only the beginning of a continued campaign of vilification. Richard may have been a dark prince but he also had undoubted qualities both as a man and a prince.

THE STANLEYS
They had a reputation of being self-seeking and seemed to have a personal hatred and contempt for Richard. In one of his letters Lord William Stanley actually dismissed Richard as 'Old Dick'. They were rewarded by Henry Tudor for their treachery at Bosworth Field. However, although related to the new King, even they were not too sure about the fate of the Princes. In 1495 Lord William Stanley paid for his treachery. He was executed for supporting Perkin Warbeck, who actually pretended to be the younger of the two Princes in the Tower.

WILLIAM CATESBY
A clever lawyer, a veritable peacock of a man. His will drawn up after Bosworth was as printed in Lovell's chronicle. Catesby may well have deferred Richard's order to execute Lord Strange in order to cultivate the Stanleys. Unfortunately they did not thank him for this, a fact Catesby alludes to in his last will and testament before he was dragged out for execution.

WILLIAM COLLINGBOURNE
One of Henry Tudor's most assiduous spies, a gentleman from Wiltshire, he composed the famous doggerel verse and pinned it up at St. Paul's. His brave death was as described in the chronicle.

HENRY PERCY, DUKE OF NORTHUMBERLAND
His conduct at Bosworth endeared him to no one. He was later assassinated whilst travelling through York (1489), an act of revenge for his gross betrayal of Richard III.

JACK OF NORFOLK

One of Richard's most trusted lieutenants, a brave, courteous man. He fought like a lion at Bosworth and his death undoubtedly led to the collapse of Richard's force. He received the famous rhyme 'Jockey of Norfolk' just before the battle. His son, Surrey, was grievously wounded but still had enough spirit to tell Henry Tudor that he would fight for any King crowned by Parliament even if it was a fence-post! Tudor, too, had his qualities: after a sojourn in the Tower, recovering from his wounds, Surrey was released.

SIR EDWARD BRAMPTON

A Portuguese Jew who converted to the Christian faith, and a staunch Yorkist. After Bosworth he went back to privateering. However, Perkin Warbeck, who later claimed to be Richard of York and engaged in a ten-year war against Henry, claimed to have been hidden in Sir Edward Brampton's retinue. Brampton may well have educated this imposter in his career as the younger of the Princes.

DUKE OF BUCKINGHAM

An overweening, ambitious nobleman. He hated the Woodvilles. As a minor he had been placed in Queen Elizabeth's household and was forced to marry one of her daughters. During the reign of Edward IV he was of little importance. Richard III, however, made the mistake of thinking that Buckingham's hatred for the Woodvilles made him a natural ally. He co-operated most closely with Richard in the *coup d'état* in the summer of 1483: there is evidence to suggest he did ask Richard for the custody of Morton, that he may well have allowed Morton to escape as well as permitting the cunning Bishop of Ely to turn his mind against Richard. I admit there is no evidence to suggest Buckingham visited the Princes in the Tower whilst Richard went on his progress in the summer of 1483, but he did remain in London. He would have had access to the Princes, he did meet Margaret Beaufort after his visit to the King at Gloucester and he seems to have had a hand in circulating the rumours about Richard being the assassin of his nephews. His rebellion, defeat and death are as described in Lovell's chronicle.

LADY MARGARET BEAUFORT

In my opinion one of Richard's most implacable and cunning of enemies, deeply pious, equally ruthless in advancing her son's claims. She and Morton were the real source of the lies against Richard such as the murder of the Princes, and the allegations that Richard had murdered his own wife in order to marry his niece. She was in London at the time of the Princes' disappearance. She did meet with Buckingham outside Gloucester and was implicated in his rebellion. Under Henry VII her chaplain, Christopher Urswicke, together with Cardinal Morton, ran Henry VII's very effective network of spies. The historian Sir George Buck mentions that Edward IV may have been poisoned and claims he saw an old chronicle which alleges that the Yorkist King was murdered by a certain Countess, perhaps the Lady Margaret. She may well have had a personal hatred for Lovell for, after Bosworth, she was given Lovell's forfeited estates.

LOUIS XI OF FRANCE, SPIDER KING OF FRANCE

His death and attempts to keep himself secure are as described in Lovell's chronicle, even to the mention of the revolving steel towers manned by bowmen.

ANN LOVELL AND HER FATHER, LORD FITZHUGH

We know very little about Anne after the battle of Bosworth in 1485 but her father was rewarded and given office by Henry Tudor shortly after Bosworth Field.

FRANCIS LOVELL, VISCOUNT TICHMARSH

Lovell was one of Richard's closest friends and lieutenants and was named in the doggerel pinned on the door of St. Paul's. However, there is some evidence that he had reservations about Richard's seizure of the throne. In his will, Catesby makes a veiled reference to this when he writes 'If the Lord Lovell be admitted to the King's Grace, (i.e. Henry Tudor) he should pray for my soul'. The other reference is the offer made to Lovell, probably of a pardon and role in the Tudor's coronation, while he was in sanctuary at Colchester. Strangely, Lovell rejected such overtures and continued to oppose Henry Tudor. He did invade England with Lincoln in 1487 and almost snatched victory at the battle of East Stoke (the place where the Irish foot-soldiers were slaughtered is still known today as 'Red Gully'). He was last seen fleeing from the battle, riding his horse across the river Trent. In 1708 a secret chamber was unearthed in his manor at Minster Lovell. The skeleton of a man was found seated at a table on which there were a book, paper and pen.

THE DEATH OF THE PRINCES

I do not want to rehearse old arguments. The Princes were last seen in the late summer of 1483. Suffice to say that Richard had no real motive for killing them. He had already usurped their position. His innocence might account for Elizabeth Woodville's capitulation to Richard in 1484. She must have been given some assurance that the man who had killed her brother, Earl Rivers, declared her marriage invalid and her sons bastard issue, had actually not killed her children. The most enigmatic question is 'Why didn't Henry Tudor, married to the Princes' sister, carry out a formal investigation?' He did not. The only thing he did was have Sir James Tyrrell executed and declare that Tyrrell murdered the Princes on Richard's orders. This is the origin of Sir Thomas More's story which must be seen as a political caricature rather than a specific description of Richard's reign

The accepted story is that the Princes' bones were found beneath some steps in the Tower during the reign of Charles II and later reinterred in Westminster Abbey However, a Dutch historian quoting Maurice, Prince of Orange, who visited England during the reign of Elizabeth I, mentions a secret room in the Tower being opened in which were found the skeletons of two young boys and which was instantly sealed up again. This room must have been in the royal apartments for a second opening of it is mentioned on the flyleaf of a 1641 edition of Thomas More's life of Richard III. These royal apartments were later pulled down under the protectorship of Oliver Cromwell 1649-1660. Cromwell's officers must have discovered the secret room and, being anti-royalist, simply dumped the bodies in a box and placed it under some stairs, where they remained until discovered in the reign of Charles II (1674).

Of course, Lovell alleges that these were the skeletons of two imposters. The idea that the Princes either escaped or were abducted from the Tower persisted right throughout the reign of Henry VII. Lambert Simnel first declared he was the younger Prince before changing his claim to being Edward of Warwick. Perkin Warbeck, who caused a great deal of trouble to Henry in the 1490s, also claimed to be Richard of York. There is no doubt of the Tudor dynasty's fear of the Yorkist cause. Henry VIII successfully wiped out all but one of the Yorkist claimants to the throne. But, to return to the original question, why didn't Henry VII proclaim the truth? The simple answer is that Henry may have been protecting someone else (his own mother), as well as avoiding a terrible dilemma; after all, he who finds the body may well be the murderer. Henry VII may have even known about the secret chamber. According to Colvin's book *The King's Works*, Henry VII carried out extensive building work in the royal apartments. Surely he must have found the secret room?

Finally, the story of Richard of Eastwell may be found in a work published in the 18th century entitled *DESIDERATA CURIOSA*. According to this, Richard Plantagenet died on 22nd December 1550 and is buried in the parish church there. Before he died, he revealed his true name to a local nobleman who was surprised to find a mason capable of reading Latin. I have followed the general outlines of this story. I believe his tomb at Eastwell can still be visited.